Gran Meccanismo

Clockpunk Roleplaying in Da Vinci's Florence

Mark Galeotti

Illustrations by Teresa Ramos

Maps by Randy Musseau

OSPREY GAMES

OSPREY GAMES
Bloomsbury Publishing Plc
Kemp House, Chawley Park, Cumnor Hill, Oxford OX2 9PH, UK
29 Earlsfort Terrace, Dublin 2, Ireland
1385 Broadway, 5th Floor, New York, NY 10018, USA
E-mail: info@ospreygames.co.uk
www.ospreygames.co.uk

OSPREY GAMES is a trademark of Osprey Publishing Ltd

First published in Great Britain in 2022

A catalogue record for this book is available from the British Library.

ISBN: HB 9781472849670; eBook 9781472849663; ePDF 9781472849649; XML 9781472849656

22 23 24 25 26   10 9 8 7 6 5 4 3 2 1

Originated by PDQ Digital Media Solutions, Bungay, UK

Printed and bound in India by Replika Press Private Ltd

Osprey Games supports the Woodland Trust, the UK's leading woodland conservation charity.

To find out more about our authors and books, visit www.ospreypublishing.com. Here you will find extracts, author interviews, details of forthcoming events and the option to sign up for our newsletter.

Illustrations by Teresa Ramos.
Maps by Randy Musseau.

The TRIPOD Game System was created by Graham Spearing
https://creativecommons.org/licenses/by/4.0/

TABLE OF CONTENTS

INTRODUCTION

"It ought to be remembered that there is nothing more difficult to take in hand, more perilous to conduct, or more uncertain in its success, than to take the lead in the introduction of a new order of things."

- Niccolò Machiavelli, The Prince

It is the Year of Our Lord 1510, and one has to wonder how differently history could have played out, wonder where we would be if Niccolò Machiavelli, the military commissioner of the Republic of Florence, had not understood the true scale of Leonardo da Vinci's genius. In such a world, the visionary might simply have wasted his time painting portraits of women and doodling in a sketchbook. How thankful we must be then, that he was provided with the opportunity to unleash our technological revolution. The New Science, of clockwork servants, high-flying gliders, water-powered cogent engines, and boundless possibilities, will inevitably and irreversibly reshape the world.

We must hope that Florence's army, now equipped with screwcopters, turtle-tanks and organ guns, will keep us secure against the armies of the Pope, Milan and the French, and that the city remains a haven for radical thinkers, artists, and other inventors inspired by da Vinci's example. However, our success has bred jealousy amongst our rival city states of the Italian peninsula – and beyond. The city's winding alleys and cobbled squares swarm with sinister Venetian spies, sour-faced priests bearing secret Papal instructions, Milanese mercenaries hoping to earn the king's ransom promised for da Vinci's secrets, not to mention the emissaries from France, England, and the Ottoman Empire with their own inscrutable agendas. These are exciting times, but dangerous ones, too. Times that challenge old understandings and assumptions. Will this new age of 'hydronetic management', of lives planned by the workings of cogent engines, free humanity or subjugate it?

Imagine a version of history where all da Vinci's inventions worked as he had hoped. What if they had been enthusiastically adopted by the powers that be and their success sparked a different kind of industrial revolution? An industrial revolution amidst the sunlit artistic ferment of the Italian Renaissance instead of the smog and fog of Victorian England. What if primitive computers, decorated with delicately painted cupids, ran on water clocks; crude, spring-powered tanks whirred across the battlefield, with cannons thundering from their flanks; and gliders flitted across perfectly blue Tuscan skies?

What could heroes get up to in this setting? One might be found drawing his rapier and preparing to duel as an army of robot knights marches past on their way to the Vatican. Another is caught up in a clash of wits with the subtle Florentine power-broker Niccolò Machiavelli. A third might be seen flirting with the notorious beauty and rumoured poisoner Lucretia Borgia. Maybe there's one plying Christopher Columbus with another drink and letting him tell them about the New World he has discovered.

Welcome to *Gran Meccanismo*, a complete and absorbing game to play with your friends set in this fantastical alternative history. *Gran Meccanismo* is a type of game known as a 'tabletop' or 'pen and paper' roleplaying game, using the simple and intuitive TRIPOD game engine set created by Graham Spearing. It is essentially a social game, a game of conversation and imagination, using descriptive phrases and translating them directly into play by giving the phrase a value, which is converted into a number of six-sided dice that you throw.

If roleplaying games are new to you, then apologies for not providing a detailed explanation of what they are. In fairness, though, it seems unlikely that, if you've bought this book, you've never been exposed to roleplaying games or you don't know someone who has. Hopefully, this section and the examples of play will give you a good sense of what's involved. More likely, though, you're familiar with the basic idea, in which case this section will give you a sense of what might be distinctive about *Gran Meccanismo* and TRIPOD.

Particular features of *Gran Meccanismo* are:

- A unique setting brings many of the tropes and dilemmas of the cyberpunk genre into a rather different and novel world.
- Free-flowing character creation guidelines allow you to describe your alter ego in the game and use those descriptions as Traits.
- This is a dice-building game: *Gran Meccanismo* requires traditional six-sided dice to play – and lots of them! Describe what your character is doing and make use of as many advantages as you can to build as large a hand or pool of dice as possible. Roll your dice and count up your successes, and the highest total wins.
- Instead of numerous complicated rules, *Gran Meccanismo* provides storytelling opportunities that are translated into Challenges. The game is meant to encourage players to give vivid descriptions that build a shared, character-focused story. Create goals for your character and drive them to succeed, playing your part in creating a fun and immersive experience for everyone.

UNITS

Although I am a devotee of the metric system, it seems more in keeping with the setting to talk in terms of miles, feet, and pounds (roughly 1.6km, 30cm, and 0.5kg, if that helps). Still, at least I am not using measurement systems contemporary to 1510, which varied from city to city or even profession to profession. A Florentine surveyor would use a *braccio* (arm) that was just under 22" long, but an engineer's braccio was 23". As for the *piede* (foot), that was some 17" in muscular Milan, but only 12" in restrained Rome.

WHAT YOU NEED TO PLAY

This book contains all of the guidance that you will need for many hours of absorbing roleplay. However, you will also need a few other things to get a game of *Gran Meccanismo* up and running. These include: two to five hours in which you and your friends can get together to play; somewhere to play; at least 12 six-sided dice; pens and paper; and some imagination. Anything else is optional.

Dice?

When the players' characters are faced with Challenges in the game's story, six-sided dice (typically referred to as d6) are rolled to help decide what happens. The number of dice that are rolled depends on the capability of the character and how favourable the circumstances are to them: the more the better.

Starter characters with good equipment, a couple of companions to help them, and some other positive factors may be able to roll up to around twelve dice. It is quite conceivable that experienced and high-powered characters with lots of helpful friends and special equipment will be able to throw sixteen or more dice when determining the outcome of challenges. It is thus well worth each player having their own set of d6. It is recommended that you buy a 'dice block' online or at specialist game stores. A block of 12mm (½") dice gives you 36, small enough that you can hold a large number in your hands.

NOW WHAT?

The standard convention for roleplaying game books is to present the rules first and then detail the world in which the game is set. *Gran Meccanismo* does things a little differently, in part reflecting the aim to emphasise that this a *storytelling* game more than a storytelling *game*. Here, the first thing is a detailed exploration of the world of *Gran Meccanismo* – above all, the pivotal city of Florence, cradle of the Renaissance. Every now and then you'll see references to Attributes or Traits or mystical numbers followed by 'd', but don't worry about them for the moment, just immerse yourself in the setting. After that, we'll discuss the rules, but they will be interspersed wherever possible with information about the world and suggestions as to how this can be turned into adventures, usually under the heading 'Story Seeds'. Extra guidance for Guides comes at the end (which is nonetheless useful for all players to read).

There Is No Exam!

What follows may seem a pretty substantial info-dump. Don't worry – you don't need to know all this. Skim it or read it in detail; the important thing is that you get some sense of the setting and the distinctive play opportunities it offers. Any phrases or ideas chime in your imagination such that you have the first glimmers of a scenario? (Organising guerrillas in Lombardy? A desperate quest to stop the Gran Meccanismo from acquiring not just sentience but self-will?) Any scenes or set pieces suggest themselves to you? (Breaking into da Vinci's fantastically trap-laden workshop to steal secret blueprints? A climactic battle hanging from the crown of the Leaning Tower of Pisa?) Any broad themes take your fancy? (Church versus New Science? Subversives preparing the ground for France's conquest of Italy?) The material in this section is background, inspiration, and reference work. When you need to know about Milanese banks or Genoese sea power, you can look it up – that's what the table of contents is for. You can change whatever you want, use whatever you want, and ignore whatever you want. The setting detail is there to help play, not to become a burden. It's your game now, after all.

What Kind of Game?

The default assumption of *Gran Meccanismo* is that the theme at the heart of play will be that this is a time of revolution, as massive changes reshape Italy and the world. However, it may be that you want to take another approach. You could play a freewheeling game of clockpunk-gizmo-festooned Florentine agents being dispatched on secret missions across Italy and beyond. Or perhaps you want to focus on Vatican politics, playing *House of Cards* in cardinals' robes. Perhaps you'd like to focus on the wars of the times, as the characters build themselves a mercenary company and lead it to death or glory. There are all kinds of ways to approach *Gran Meccanismo*, which the Guide chapter discusses in more detail (p. 165).

Deep in the bowels of the Palazzo Altoviti, mathematician, philosopher, and reluctant State Clocker Second Class Riccardo Buri and his protégé, Claudia Petracci, know they only have a few minutes whilst the main Supervisory Apparatus's water reservoirs are refilled to tap into the Gran Meccanismo via one of its primary terminals in order to get it to spit out new Catalogo cards for them, granting them new identities and new lives.

THE WORLD OF GRAN MECCANISMO

"The vulgar always is taken by appearances, and the world consists chiefly of the vulgar."

- Niccolò Machiavelli, The Prince

The glider banks gently, the bright red fleur-de-lis on its broad canvas wings showing to all that it is a courier of the Florentine Republic. Cradled on the warm winds of a Tuscan summer, it soars serenely along the course of the River Arno.

Below, the sprawling patchwork of traditional fields gives way to the broad state farms of Peretola, where hundreds of unransomed soldiers, the spoils of the recent defence of Pisa from the Milanese, labour in chain gangs, feeding the mighty grain mills that grind and groan morning, noon and night to feed the masses of the sprawling new Florence. They are the lucky ones, though, the ones deemed likely to be ransomed. The less fortunate are breaking their backs far to the west, digging out the new harbour basins outside Pisa where da Vinci's rumoured new screwships are to be built.

At least they can feel the sun on their backs, though. As it approaches its destination, the glider gently descends. Below, faces turn upwards from the winding alleys of Firenze Fuorimuri, the sprawling suburbs of cheap flophouses and officine – workshops that have grown up to service the artisanal revolution now gripping the city. At its heart, behind incongruously cheery whitewashed walls, is Le Gigli, the infamous labour-prison where enemies of the state toil until they drop on the winding machines, coiling the mass-produced springs that drive so many of the new contraptions, like the automatic looms that click and clack below.

As it approaches the warm red walls of Florence itself, the glider banks more sharply, angling to one side. After all, not even a courier may fly above the city itself. On one of the tower walls, a siege crossbow idly tracks the glider, but its chimney merely steams gently. If its gunners anticipated action, they would frantically be throwing wood into the firebox to heat up the boiler, but they seem just to be checking the gearing of the mount. Florence may be at war, but this is a lazy mid-afternoon and the city is comfortable, complacent even, in its unexpected pre-eminence.

With an adept tug of the control ropes, the pilot twists the flaps on the glider's birdlike wings and brings it down to a neat landing at the Aliantodrome just outside the walls (and beneath the guns of Fort Belvedere). The ground crews, ready for his arrival, are promptly at his side, and a sealed message tube is handed on to the waiting horseman. Some day he may be riding one of these new-fangled two-wheeled spring-horses, but for now a flesh-and-blood mount is best for clattering through the city's winding cobbled streets. Within less than ten minutes, the Signoria, the city's governing council, will learn what terms Milan has accepted...

HOW HYSTERICAL IS THIS HISTORY?

Set aside the admittedly not-so-minor details as clockwork computers and steam-powered crossbows, and the answer is that this is a setting soundly based on history as seems most fun – frankly, the real era in which *Gran Meccanismo* takes place is interesting in and of itself. That said, some things have been changed, especially where altering a detail or moving something by a year or two makes the setting more entertaining. The Order of St John was only given Malta in 1530, for example, and Savonarola actually only lived until 1498. Of course, the virtue of this is that it makes it all the more easy and appropriate for you to tweak the history as you want, too.

THE RENAISSANCE

The Renaissance – or Rinascimento in Italian – is a period of extraordinary social, political, artistic, and economic change across Europe, focused first in Italy and spreading outwards from there, roughly across the fifteenth and sixteenth centuries. In the fourteenth century, famine and the Black Death had decimated the population, the Church was torn by the Western Schism, the poor rose against their feudal masters, and superstition and ignorance were rife. But Europe survived, and a phoenix was about to be born in the Italian city state of Florence. This was a time when suddenly art, politics, business, and philosophy were flourishing, hand in hand. A new class of bankers and merchants was challenging the still-powerful feudal lords, whose wealth was based on land and warfare. Wars were still fought, and often, but rivalries were just as frequently expressed in the realms of patronage and display, as the rich and the powerful competed to show that they were more cultured, elegant, and educated than their rivals.

The revelation that the much-feted daredevil pilot 'Paulo Ziani' is actually Paula Ziani, the estranged daughter of a Venetian nobleman, has led to a new clamour for women to be inducted into Florence's glider corps.

ITALY

Italy is a patchwork of republics, city states, and principalities. The territories of the Most Illustrious Florentine Republic stretch across north-western Italy, its lands becoming reshaped by canals, roads, and industry as it goes through a scientific and philosophical revolution driven by luminaries such as Leonardo da Vinci and Niccolò Machiavelli, under the rule of Gonfaloniere (in effect, President) Piero Soderini. The Republics of Lucca and Siena are now subjects of Florence, their governing councils little more than vassals of the 'envoys' sent to 'advise' them, their young men increasingly lured away by the new opportunities of Florence.

To the north, Milan is technically under French control, albeit loosely, despite the guerrilla war being fought by the remnants of the old order. Once, Milan considered itself the rising power of Italy, and although its forces were recently humbled by the murderous marvels of Florence's technological revolution, Milan is determined that it will rise again.

Squeezed between rising Florence and jealous Milan, its traditional maritime power increasingly undermined by Florence's plans to build fleets of screwships to force passage into the Atlantic and then to exploit the New World, Genoa finds itself offered a choice of masters. For now, Rome thinks it dominates the famous trading city, but which way will the back-biting and divided consuls of Genoa really jump?

To the south, the Papal States are implacable foes of Florence, seeing its Great November Revolution and subsequent humanist movement as nothing less than a Satanic plot. But the fiery Pope Julius II is almost equally suspicious of Venice, and thus plots with Milan and the French, dreaming of returning all Italy to his dominion. Who amongst the priests and good Catholics of Italy are his – and the feared Inquisition's – spies and saboteurs?

Further south, the Kingdoms of Naples and Sicily are Spanish puppet-states. At present, Florence and Spain compete for the Mediterranean behind the scenes, each backing privateers who loot the other's shipping, but one day the turtle-tanks and musketeers of Florence will face the feared Spanish infantry for mastery of the land, too.

However, the Venetian Republic is perhaps Florence's greatest rival, its treasury full of the profits of its mighty trading empire, its territories and stations stretching around the Mediterranean. The languid beauty of *La Serenissima* (the Most Serene One), as Venice is known, has a heart of ice, with the agents of the governing Council of Ten's State Inquisition being the most feared spies and secret police in all Europe, and the Venetian navy even able to challenge the looming power of the Muslim Ottoman Empire.

HOLY
ROMAN
EMPIRE

Torino

Milan

Occupied
Verona

Venice

Trieste

Mantua

Padua

Genoa

Parma

Ferrara

Bologna

Carrara

Ravenna

Lucca

Florence

San Marino

Pisa

San Gimignano

Urbino

FRANCE

Ligurian
Sea

Siena

Assisi

Ancona

Adriatic
Sea

Corsica

Rome

Kingdom of
Naples

Sardinia

Tyrrhenian
Sea

Naples

Salerno

Otranto

Ionian
Sea

ITALY
1510
ANNO DOMINI

Palermo

Kingdom of
Sicily

Mediterranean
Sea

FLORENCE:
CRADLE OF THE RENAISSANCE

All cities have their day, and this is definitely Florence's – suddenly finding itself at the forefront of not just the cultural, artistic, and social rebirth of the Renaissance, but also the sudden emergence of the New Science. This is not just tilting the balance of power in Italy and beginning an industrial revolution in Tuscany's towns and valleys; it is also raising fundamental questions about power, society, and even humanity.

Quite how this happened is detailed in the section unpacking this crucial city (p. 37), but for now suffice it to say that at present it is a city in ferment, a place where new ideas, from technological developments to artistic breakthroughs, are emerging every day. Water-powered looms and assembly lines are galvanising Florence's industries, rapid-firing organ guns and armoured turtle-tanks are making it a pocket-sized military superpower, gliders scud across its skies and paddle-steamers haul cargoes along its rivers. It's not just about technology – all the old dogmas and prejudices are coming under question: Florentine priests openly debate whether the Vatican has become corrupt; long-standing laws against the Jews are being re-examined or simply ignored; women are beginning to be admitted into universities in ever-larger numbers; and a pauper with a bankable idea is as likely as a nobleman to get investors.

Such a revolution is not without its dark side, however. Some worry that this is making Florence too powerful to ignore, yet not powerful enough to survive. Pope Julius II considers the New Science to be a Satanic design. Milan, whose forces suffered a humiliating defeat at Florentine hands at the battle for Pisa last year, is out for revenge. Venice spies a new rival. Even France, for all that Gonfaloniere Soderini is a friend, looks at Florence's new wealth and ponders what it would cost to take it. The challenge is also more fundamental. Is change simply happening too quickly for its implications to be properly considered? The new water-clock and spring-driven cogent engines have not just revolutionised business and industry: the Gran Meccanismo, mightiest of them all, promises to usher in a new era of uniformity and control. Already, every Florentine citizen is meant to carry their Catalogo identity card at all times. The apostles of hydronetic management theory look to a future of maximum efficiency, but to what extent will efficiency be bought at the cost of humanity?

Guide's Notes

Whilst games need not be set in Florence, the city is the axis on which the world of *Gran Meccanismo* turns, the source of its weird and wonderful clockpunk gizmos, the destabilising factor driving trade wars, social revolution, religious debate, and bloody conflict. If the cyberpunk fantasies we know well tend to be about rain, neon and video adverts, Japanese script, and skyscrapers, then this clockpunk aesthetic is sunlit and Italian, defined by clacking water-driven computers in finely-etched bronze, crude steam engines alongside ox-carts, elegant palazzos suddenly sprouting semaphore towers, and erratic – quite possibly explosive – new inventions, decorated with cherubs and gargoyles.

Iconic scenes would include crossing the hills above Florence and suddenly seeing the city spread out below around the huge and glorious Duomo, or cathedral, with its tall, square-edged bell tower; walking through da Vinci's workshop, like a sixteenth-century version of Q's in a Bond movie, as apprentices test crucifixes that fire poison darts and a self-driving cart; an impromptu debate in the square in front of the Church of Santa Maria Novella, as a traditionalist priest and a radical monk swap scripture and insults in front of a crowd of the curious and the partisan.

PARLIAMO ITALIANO

Be assured: you don't need to speak Italian to play *Gran Meccanismo*. That said, there are a lot of Italian names and words that will be thrown around, so here is the absolute basic guide. Pronunciation notes for key words and names are provided through the text.

On pronunciation, probably the biggest issue is the humble letter c. In Italian, a *ch* is a hard c, like a k, whilst a *c* is usually a ch, unless it's before an a, o, or u. Double cs are also ch. So hunter, *cacciatore*, is ka-chya-tor-ay, and church, *chiesa*, is kee-air-sa. Oh, and the *g*? It's usually a hard g, although sometimes it's a soft j, or is even silent when followed by an i, so the name Guglielmo is gool-ee-elmo. But honestly, if no one round the table knows better, it's no big deal, and on the whole the rest of the alphabet sounds as you'd expect.

Italian plurals generally end in -i or -e, so *cacciatori* or *chiese*. You only need to know that to recognise that in occasional use in the book, where a word ends in -i or -e, it's probably a plural.

And that's it! It's a lovely language, but unless you really fancy a new hobby, you don't need to learn any more of it.

Pope Julius II is determined to crush Florence and the New Science. And Venice. And the French. And anyone else who gets in his way.

ROME: CITY OF THE CHURCH

The Eternal City is no longer the largest in Italy – it is home to just 50,000 souls, fewer than Florence's 75,000 or Milan's, Naples's, or Venice's 100,000 – but it fstill feels huge, as its people still live within the vestiges of the imperial capital of centuries past. This is a city of contrasts – squalid slums next to glittering palaces, the grandiose ruins of the ancient empire juxtaposed with the ambitious designs of the Church. Just take a look at the Vatican, on the west bank of the Tiber River. The soaring grandeur of St Peter's Basilica is proof of both its spiritual status and its cultural patronage, with the great artist Michelangelo still painting the ceiling of the Sistine Chapel of the Pope's Apostolic Palace. The Vatican Apostolic Library speaks to the Church's role as a guardian of knowledge. One of the oldest libraries in the world, it is home to a vast selection of books, from biblical translations to profane works kept under lock and key. The Castle St Angelo was originally built by the Roman emperor Hadrian but is now a Papal fortress, a reminder that the Church is also a ruthless imperial power, whose armies enforce Vatican rule across the Papal States. It, and the Apostolic Palace, are guarded by the elite Swiss Guard, newly formed by Pope Julius II.

This Pope is a proud, ambitious, and capable man. He has put his hand to both public works and aggressive statecraft, and it is beginning to show in Rome. New churches are being built, but there are also fountains from which the poor may drink, and charitable missions offering bread and cheese. Even so, this is largely a dirty and dangerous city in which fortunes can be lost as easily as made, and life is often ugly and brief. But the idea of Rome, the city that spans this world and the next, the treasury of Christendom and the seat of religious learning – that dream endures.

The Pope directly rules over a stretch of central Italy. Under the martial Julius II, the Vatican has also extended effective control over the duchies of Perugia, Bologna, Spoleto, and Romagna. There are local governments, but they owe vassalage, tax, and military service to Rome. The Marches are also regarded as part of the Papal States, although in practice real power in this troublesome hill country is still in the hands of all manner of local warlords and city assemblies.

Guide's Notes

Rome should be played as a city of contrasts. It's a violent and often squalid place for most, who live in the shadow of Roman ruins, outside the hallowed precincts of the Vatican or the high, guarded walls of the noble town estates. Street gangs, revolutionary cabals, and desperation are the order of the day in the slums, with intrigue and indulgence rife amongst the noble and Church elite. Indeed, if you want to include a Renaissance equivalent of the Mafia, it is Rome, not Sicily, where it will be found.

Iconic scenes would include Julius II delivering a powerful peroration in the huge expanse of St Peter's Square; shady deals being struck in the shadow of the ruined Colosseum, knives in hand; following a conspirator who is heading down into the trackless passages of the Roman catacombs.

VENICE: LA SERENISSIMA

The rich island city of Venice, with its canals and gondolas, masked balls, and delicate architecture, might seem a romantic, even magical place. It's even called The Most Serene Republic, La Serenissima. And it is, but only because of the ruthless, cold-eyed determination of its lords that keeps it so. Venice is also known for its extensive overseas territories – the slice of neighbouring Italy called the Terraferma, including the subject cities of Brescia, Padua, and (until its recent conquest by the Holy Roman Empire) Verona, as well as islands and cities along the Dalmatian coast. It keeps those by its formidable navy, built in the advanced production line of the Arsenale, and the most feared and sophisticated secret police in the world. On the face of it, the Venetian Inquisition (nothing to do with the Church's Holy Inquisition) is the investigative magistracy of the republic – spy-catchers and thief-takers. But it also has a network of spies and assassins, across Italy and beyond, that everyone fears if they have any sense at all.

Power is in the hands of a pragmatic ruling class of merchants, bankers, and aristocrats. They elect the 2000 members of the Great Council, who have no real duties but in turn to elect the people who really run the Venetian Republic – the Council of Ten and the Doge. This last position is the executive leader of the state, elected for life, and the current Doge, Leonardo Loredan, is an energetic and ruthless schemer, as befits the times. However, Venice is at odds with Pope Julius II – who has excommunicated the city for seizing Papal territories – and has just lost lands to the French and the Holy Roman Empire in their latest foray into Italy. It is also still recovering from a hard-fought war with its main challenger for dominance of the eastern Mediterranean, the Ottoman Empire. Its control of the lucrative spice trade is under question, and there are faint, troubling indications of future decline. Doge Loredan knows he must do something to reverse this trend, whether through war, diplomacy, or perhaps – given that Rome is already an enemy – the New Science?

After all, Venice has its own technological strengths. The glassblowers of the island of Murano are so famous and skilled that they live in a gilded cage, forbidden to take their skills elsewhere on pain of being hunted down by Venetian assassins. The powerful guilds of the city foster much invention in fields from printing to chemistry. And, of course, the Republic is rich in gold (the Venetian ducat is one of the best-regarded coins in Europe), as well as tradecraft and guile. What the Florentines may not want to share with a potential ally, they may be willing to sell; and what they may not want to sell, Venetian spies can steal. With a fleet of steam-powered ironclads and submarines, with an army fielding turtle-tanks and clockwork organ guns, who could challenge La Serenissima?

Guide's Notes

Imagine a fairy city meets the KGB. On the surface, everything is beautiful, prosperous, and carefree, but there's always a paranoid and calculating edge. Around the city are the stone 'post boxes', called the Lion's Mouths, into which Venetians can drop anonymous denunciations. Sometimes, someone might be grabbed by the Inquisition in the middle of St Mark's Square, the huge and bustling heart of the city, and everyone will simply pretend not to notice. In games, the Venetians could be the Cold War Soviets of *Gran Meccanismo*, the distant antagonists whose espionage networks and cold-hearted assassins are a constant threat.

Iconic scenes would include a black-shrouded funeral barge being silently rowed along a foggy canal; a freshly built war galley setting out from the Arsenale; the great bronze figures on the clock tower in St Mark's Square tolling the hour; a snatch of laughter and music as the great main door of a palazzo opens to let more guests into a masked ball; a team of heavyset men in anonymous workers' clothes arresting a protesting foreigner with taciturn efficiency.

THE OPIUM TRADE

Opium is a widely used painkiller, so one of the aspects of the 'Voyages of Discovery' was the quest to find new sources and control the existing trade routes to India. Historically, Venice has been able to control the overland routes, but since the Portuguese Vasco de Gama discovered a sea route to India around the Cape of Good Hope, Lisbon has begun to make inroads into the trade. Will Venice be willing to accept the loss of its opium trade and simply buy it from the Portuguese like everyone else? It cannot prevent Portugal's fleets from taking the Cape route, so may instead have to try to make its land routes cheaper or safer, something which would require improved relations with the Ottoman Empire. Or maybe it will look to growing its own, which would require new territorial expansion for fields and labour-intensive poppy farming.

MILAN: GLORY AND OCCUPATION

Once a republic, the Lombard city of Milan was conquered in 1450 by the mercenary captain Francesco Sforza, and for the next half century his dynasty made it the well-run powerhouse of northern Italy. Rich, cultured, and thriving, it was a tempting prize for France. In 1494, Ludovico Sforza, known as Ludovico the Moor, made a fateful misstep when he allied with the French against a new threat from King Alfonso II of Naples and Pope Alexander VI. Milan allowed French armies through its territories on their way to attack Naples, but Charles VIII of France then laid claim to Milan, too. Ludovico desperately turned to Maximilian, the Holy Roman Emperor. Charles eventually withdrew from Italy, but when his successor, Louis XII, returned in vengeance, none of the other city states would help defend the city that had involved the French in Italian politics in the first place. In 1500, Milan fell.

Louis has added 'Duke of Milan' to his existing titles, but he remains in Paris. Instead, the city is under the rule of Governor Gian Giacomo Trivulzio, once one of Ludovico's trusted aides, now on the payroll of the French. Trivulzio is as able an administrator as a general, but his greed means that he is trying to squeeze every ducat he can from the lands under his control, whilst buying fine art and living like a king. Paris is far away, after all, and although there are some French officials and a contingent of their Swiss mercenaries in Milan, on the whole power is still in the hands of the Lombard aristocracy, who are more than happy to exploit their people and blame King Louis. Away from the city, Milan's lands are increasingly being carved up into semi-independent fiefdoms, like the lands of the Borromeo family of bankers around Lake Maggiore. Trivulzio is well aware of this, but he cannot risk turning against the aristocracy. Not today, anyway.

In a bid to demonstrate his value to Paris and also gain a lucrative new holding, last year Trivulzio sent Milanese forces into Tuscany to try and help the city of Pisa resist Florence. The result was a humiliation, and a demonstration of the power of Florence's New Science on the battlefield. Trivulzio was left in debt, in trouble with the French, and in no doubt that his and Milan's future depend somehow on neutralising upstart Florence.

For all that, Milan is still one of the richest cities in Italy. The angular, red-brick Sforza Castle at the heart of the city, now the governor's residence, is a marvel of modern military architecture, bristling with cannon. Its banks finance ventures across Europe. Yet life is getting harder, the courts no longer protect the commoner against the whim and extortion of the governor's cronies, and the gold-on-blue fleurs-de-lis of the French is now part of Milan's flag. No wonder there is a simmering undercurrent of dissatisfaction in the city, and often outright rebellion in the countryside. Ludovico's 17-year-old son Massimiliano, by all accounts a feckless youth in reality, has become a folk hero, the people's hope and inspiration. No one knows for sure where he is, but rumours abound – he is raising an army of clockwork soldiers in Florence with which to liberate Milan; he is under cover in the city, ready to challenge Trivulzio to a duel; he is a secret captive, bricked up inside the Sforza Castle; he is nowhere, and thus somehow seemingly everywhere.

Guide's Notes

Milan fills two roles in *Gran Meccanismo*. On the one hand, it is another of the big players of Italian power politics. It may be a French territory, but until Louis visits or becomes concerned with what's going on, it's essentially still an Italian city, with Trivulzio its duke in all but name. However, Trivulzio has his own ambitions, and any triumphs he can achieve will either raise his stock in Paris or, as some dare to whisper, may even allow him to throw off French domination. So, he's an ambitious, risk-taking operator, who could be behind any plot, whether to steal New Science, hijack Venetian tax convoys, or rig the election of the next Pope. The other role is as a potential site for rabble-rousing and rebellion. Milan could be played like a city under occupation – Vichy Paris, say – with cells of revolutionaries gathering in garrets and plotting their next move whilst Trivulzio's spies and Swiss mercenaries track them down, or with the towns and villages of Lombardy home to a Robin Hood-style rural insurgency.

Iconic scenes would include: the grand Duomo of Milan, started in 1386 and still not yet complete, but nonetheless the largest church in all Italy; a platoon of dour Swiss mercenaries marching out of the Sforza Castle for a dawn patrol of the city; the riotous Feast of St Ambrose (Milan's patron saint) held on 7th December, when the nobility compete to put on the most lavish displays of their wealth, from fireworks to tables in the street groaning with food for all-comers.

STORY SEED: BRING ME THE HEAD OF SYLVESTER II

Gerbert of Aurillac, who ascended to the Papacy as Sylvester II in 999, was a scholar and a scientist. He brought Arabic numerals to Europe, reintroduced the abacus, and generally combined science and faith. Legend has it that he built a brass head that was able to answer questions with a simple yes or no, possessed by a demoness called Meridiana. Sylvester was buried in St John Lateran Cathedral in Rome, but his construct was lost. Until now. Rumours have begun to spread of an itinerant prophet travelling the back country of Calabria, the toe of Italy's boot. He predicts the end of days, in dialogue with an ancient brass head. Gerbert was a master of both mechanics and numbers – he built a small brass-piped organ that could mimic human speech; could he also have built an early cogent engine that could mimic thought? Is this the Brass Head of Pope Sylvester II? Or is it merely the work of a charlatan? It's little wonder that Gonfaloniere Soderini is interested, seeing it as a possible interface for the *Gran Meccanismo*, and has sent agents to acquire it. It's also unsurprising that the Vatican, horrified by any suggestion that a Pope could be an ancestor of the blasphemous New Science, is offering a generous bounty to whomever can recover the head. But why is the Genoese scholar-adventurer Filippo Malfante also after the head? Zealots, clockers, archaeologists, and bounty-hunters clash in a race for the artefact.

GENOA: TRADING NATION

One of the great trading centres of the age, the port city of Genoa is known for its sailors, merchants, explorers, and mercenaries. There is even a Latin phrase, *Genuensis ergo mercator*, meaning 'a Genoese and therefore a merchant'. Christopher Columbus came from Genoa, and so too have many of the other leading voyagers and cartographers of the age, such as Giovanni Caboto – known as John Cabot – who recently travelled to North America for Henry VII of England.

Genoa currently possesses a network of trading stations from the Black Sea to Lisbon, rivalled only by the that of the Venetians. Two of the oldest banks in the world, the Bank of St George and the Banca Carige, were founded here. Nor are they afraid to fight, though even then, there is an entrepreneurial angle – the much-feared mercenary companies of Genoese crossbowmen have fought from Crécy to Jerusalem, from naval operations in the Mediterranean to campaigns in southern Russia. Under its famous admiral Andrea Doria, the Genoese fleet scours the Mediterranean both of Barbary pirates from North Africa and of Turkish shipping, bringing its prizes back for sale in Genoa's markets.

Under off-and-on French control since 1458, Genoa has just been liberated by forces led by Genoese nobleman Giano II di Campofregoso, much of whose army was raised with Papal funds. He is nonetheless struggling with jealous rival families and dogged by claims that he is simply a puppet of the Vatican. Some even say it would be better to submit to distant Spain than all-too-close Rome – or even turn to Florence. It is rumoured that somewhere in the city is the lost last manuscript of Leon Battista Alberti, the fourteenth-century Genoese polymath with a particular talent for cryptography, whose elegant algorithms could speed up Florence's cogent engines – or break them.

The city is unsurprisingly dominated by its broad harbour and overlooked by a tall lighthouse painted with the city's coat of arms, atop of which a lantern fuelled by olive oil lights the night. Much of the city is still medieval in form, threaded by narrow and winding alleys, but with the money rolling in from far-flung trading and banking ventures, the oligarch-noblemen of Genoa are already beginning to contemplate ambitious reconstruction, demolishing some of the worse slums to build glorious new palaces connected by wide, modern thoroughfares.

Guide's Notes

If characters want to buy something, sell something, or get somewhere, Genoa is the place to be. Part Casablanca, part trading emporium, in *Gran Meccanismo* it is the place where anyone can go to meet anyone else. It could also be the starting point for adventures set further afield – empire-building in the New World, trading ventures to the Indies, a diplomatic mission to the Ottoman court, or even exploring southern Russia from the Black Sea.

Iconic scenes would include a fleet returning to port, some ships barely still afloat, others loaded high with plunder and prisoners; a final battle atop the lighthouse, both fighters trying to fling the other over the parapet; the sights, sounds, and smells of the waterfront markets, as stall-holders clamour for attention, with goods from across the known world.

NAPLES: SPANISH OUTPOST

Founded by the Greeks in the eighth century BC, Naples is one of the oldest cities in Italy, and a gateway through which Greek, Arab, and Ottoman ideas have entered the European mainstream. Its location in the south of Italy has meant that it has always felt different, and indeed it is. Since 1442, Naples has been a possession of the Spanish King of Aragon, despite brief periods (1495–6 and 1501–4) under French rule. From his seat of power in the mighty, twin-towered Castel Nuovo, Alfonso I of Naples – Alfonso V of Aragon – began to transform this sprawling and impoverished city. Artists were invited to Naples, libraries were established and a magnificent arch was built to span the main gate of Castel Nuovo. The Kingdom of Naples is now part of the territories of King Ferdinand II, the first ruler of a united Spain, but he has entrusted it to his viceroy, Ramón de Cardona, whom many believe to be the king's illegitimate son. The kingdom extends across most of southern Italy, as well as the islands of Sicily and Sardinia. This is the largest territory in all of Italy, albeit by no means the richest or most advanced.

Guide's Notes

The Kingdom of Naples is a rolling backwater, a land where a few cities sit like islands of relative prosperity and modernity amidst an impoverished countryside where life has scarcely changed for centuries. Characters in the sun-baked south may feel their circumstances are more like those of a 'spaghetti Western' *Gran Meccanismo* compared with the more urban and urbane adventures in the north.

The kingdom is also an outpost of Spanish power. Italy's tragedy is that, divided, it is all too often a battlefield fought over by the great powers of France and Spain – although the rising power of Florence may yet change that. Although Viceroy de Cardona is not an especially harsh or religious man, he is more a general than a governor and rumour has it that he is soon to be given orders to muster an army, reinforced by tough Spanish infantry, with which to march north. Whilst he would want his wife, Doña Isabel de Requesens, to rule in his place, he could be replaced as Viceroy by Cardinal Francisco de Remolins. A zealot, de Remolins would bring the Spanish Inquisition and a new iron rule to Naples, which might breed rebellion or make Naples an increasingly dangerous player in the politics of the age.

Lucrezia Borgia is now Lucrezia d'Este, but still a fabled beauty and subtle schemer. Still, the rumours that she is also a mistress of poisons and philtres are no doubt false. No doubt.

OTHER MAIN CITIES

One of the main seaports in the Marches, **Ancona** looks out onto the Adriatic and has a proud tradition of independence. Under increasing pressure from Rome, its autonomy is shrinking, but individual Anconitans are as proud and bloody-minded as ever.

There is no greater seat of learning than the university in **Bologna**, the oldest in the world. Red-walled Bologna was taken by Papal troops in 1506, and remains subject to Rome, although begrudgingly. Papal legate Francesco Alidosi is still struggling to impose his authority on the city's feuding noble families, many of whom still live in the fortified medieval towers that stud the city. The Basilica of San Petronio is the largest brick cathedral in the world, and it may be the pride they feel that helps explain why its clergy have tended to side with the free-thinking university rather than the Papal legate, who grumbles about 'Florentine influences' and is starting to draw up a list of names.

The dusty township of **Carrara**, part of the Duchy of Massa and Carrara, ruled by the Malaspina family, is nestled in the foothills of the Apennine Mountains. Its marble quarries produce the finest-quality stone in the world, much prized by sculptors and builders across Italy and beyond.

Ferrara is a centre of learning, its university amongst the finest in Europe, but it maintains its independence thanks to both its advanced, extensive fortifications and its foundries – Ferrarese cannon are considered Italy's best. It is ruled by Duke Alfonso d'Este and his dangerously beautiful wife Lucrezia, once Borgia. For Alfonso's willingness to deal with the French (as well as because the Pope despises his old enemies, the Borgias, and all associated with them), Julius II has just excommunicated Alfonso and declared his land forfeit to the Papacy. However, Alfonso is not just a noted patron of the arts; he is a competent military commander and a more than competent ruler. His reply? 'The Pope can come and take my lands.' Julius II intends to take him up on the challenge, and soon, so Ferrara is arming. Another of the d'Este cities, **Modena**, looks set to be first on the Pope's list.

The Republic of **Lucca** is just about holding on to its independence, although it is virtually a Florentine protectorate by now. The Florentines have offered steam crossbows to help reinforce its walls, and a brand-new clock for its clock tower – the tallest construction in the town – but at what price?

Surrounded on all sides by artificial lakes, the Lombard city of **Mantua** is known as one of the most cultured in all Italy. Marquis Francesco II Gonzaga is a *condottiere*, or mercenary, commander of legendary prowess and bravery, but the real driving force for the cultural life of Mantua is his wife, Isabella d'Este. She is a prolific letter-writer, and her correspondents range from the King of France to a network of leading women of the age. Last year, Francesco was captured by the Venetians whilst fighting for the French. In his absence, Isabella – sister of Alfonso of Ferrara – has been ruling as regent, even commanding Mantua's forces when the city was besieged by the Holy Roman Empire.

Despite a recent siege by the forces of the Holy Roman Empire, **Padua** remains a Venetian holding, under two officials elected from the Venetian nobility, a *podestà* (mayor) and a captain in charge of its garrison. This is an enlightened imperialism, though, and Padua's own laws and local administration are largely left in peace. Indeed, the Venetians are spending money on the city, raising impressive new walls and a palace for the podestà, so the city is going through something of a building boom and builders from across Italy are heading there for work.

The Sicilian city of **Palermo** has been controlled by everyone from the Arabs to the Phoenicians, and now is the capital of the Spanish-ruled Kingdom of Sicily, where Viceroy Hugo of Moncada sits in the Norman Palace, albeit subordinate to Viceroy de Cardona in Naples. From the heavy-set fortress of Castellamare, a massive chain stretches across the harbour, its other end being anchored at the Church of Santa Maria della Catena (St Mary of the Chain). Those who worry about the impact of Spanish rule in Naples should perhaps look across the Tyrrhenian Sea to Sicily, where the Holy Inquisition is increasingly visible and Jews are being expelled.

Once a great maritime republic, the port city of **Pisa** has fallen on hard times. It used the French invasion of 1494 to claim independence from Florence, but has since been recaptured. Now its nobles are being supplanted by agents of the Signoria, and its workers are being dragooned into the construction of a new harbour and covered shipyard, whispered to be where a whole new type of vessel will be built. The famous leaning tower, the freestanding bell tower of Pisa's cathedral, is being taken by the disgruntled Pisans as a symbol of their plight: 'we must lean, but we do not fall'.

Ravenna is a city with a glorious past and an uncertain present. For almost a century, it was the capital of the Western Roman Empire, then the Ostrogothic Kingdom, and later a Byzantine stronghold. Annexed by Venice in 1441, last year Vatican armies took the city and imposed a Papal legate as governor. Nonetheless, the city and its lands are in turmoil, not least because of the news of a monstrous birth; a child allegedly born of the sinful union of a nun and a monk, with a horned head, a goat's leg, and an eye on its right knee. The child was promptly put to death, its body burnt and its ashes washed away with holy water. Nonetheless, this is widely considered a sign of great and terrible change. The Church has declared it proof of the Satanic influences of the New Science, whilst Ravennans have taken it as evidence of the illegitimacy of Papal invasion. In Brancaleone Castle, Obizzo Alidosi, brother of Francesco Alidosi, paces the battlements at night, terrified of what the next day may bring, whilst his soldiers and servants cross themselves when he passes and mutter about his state of mind.

The walled hill-town of **San Gimignano** (Jim-in-YAH-no) is a gem of medieval architecture, with a score of tall, square-based towers dominating its skyline. It has been a Florentine possession since the fourteenth century, when the Black Death decimated its population. Now, its towers attract experimental glider engineers keen to test new designs, and scientists keen to learn the secrets of the heavens with their new telescopes, fitted with lenses ground by cogent engines to hitherto-impossible accuracy.

Under the dictatorial rule of Pandolfo Petrucci, a man who has weathered invasions, conspiracies, and even his father-in-law's attempt to murder him, the Republic of **Siena** nonetheless prospers. Petrucci is a wily and ruthless man (even rumoured to have had Pope Pius III poisoned) who plays off France against Spain, Florence against Rome, and the Sienese people against the noble families. However, with Siena increasingly falling into Florence's orbit, it's an open question whether Petrucci will accept this or pull off another realignment. Siena isn't lacking in assets – Siena University is famous, the Monte dei Paschi is one of Italy's largest banks, and the city controls silver and copper mines and a lucrative salt industry. However, it is best known for the contests between the city's 17 *contrade*, or wards. The main square is the site of bouts of *pugna*, 'punch', essentially a public brawl in which a champion of each contrada struggles to be the last man standing whilst crowds of rival supporters cheer and jeer, or else run races across the breadth of the city whilst partisans of the other wards try to trip or otherwise block them.

Although the French town of Chambéry is the capital of the trans-Alpine Duchy of Savoy, the Italian city of **Torino** (Turin) is larger and more significant, something the Torinesi never fail to point out, begrudging the greater status of the French over the Lombard Italians. Indeed, many quietly support the rebels in neighbouring Milan, and if Massimiliano ever does topple Trivulzio, then that may be just the spark needed to trigger a Lombard uprising in Savoy, too. The university, known for its strengths in law and medicine, is a particular hotbed of unrest.

The cultured city of **Urbino**, in the Papal-controlled Marches, was ruled by Cesare Borgia, illegitimate son of Pope Alexander VI, until 1507. Since his death, it has been the dukedom of Francesco Maria I della Rovere, nephew of the current Pope, Julius II, which tells you much about the politics of the time. He is a condottiere of some renown, and a captain-general of the Papal armies, married to Eleonora Gonzaga, daughter of Francesco Gonzaga of Mantua and an elegant and gracious patron of the arts.

Once a Milanese possession, then a Venetian one, **Verona** is currently under the control of the Holy Roman Empire, from whence Emperor Maximilian plans to extend Habsburg rule across northern Italy. The medieval stronghold of Castelvecchio is now home to a regiment of elite Landsknechte pikemen, and the real power in the city rests with their captain, Heinrich von Tiefenbach, not the city council that still meets in the elegant Loggia del Consiglio palace.

GUELFS AND GHIBELLINES

One of the defining political divides that once cut across all Italy – through cities, factions, and even families – is that between the Guelfs and the Ghibellines. This feud is 300 years old and, like so many lasting disputes, has become a matter of tradition as much as anything else, with old grudges handed down from father to son. Very broadly, the dispute is about who should have ultimate authority over Italy – the Guelfs support the Pope and the Ghibellines the Holy Roman Emperor. Whilst this feud has been in decline, the turmoil of the Florentine revolution has given it a new relevance. Two hundred years ago, Florence was a Guelf city, but saw a split between the Black Guelphs, rich merchants who still supported Papal power, and the White Guelfs, who, drawn from the poorer citizenry, mistrusted Pope and Emperor alike.

Florence largely ignores the Guelf-Ghibelline question, but the Guelfs in Italy are still loyal to the Pope and thus tend also to mistrust the New Science. Because they fear the prospect of the Holy Roman Empire seizing Italy and forcing the Pope to subordinate himself to the Emperor, they are also inclined to favour the French, who are presently the Empire's main rival. Conversely, the Ghibellines see the Empire as Italy's potential saviour, despising what they see as the corruption and backwardness of Papal rule. By extension, they are, if not supportive of Florence itself, at least interested in the technological and philosophical fruits of its revolution.

Main Ghibelline cities include Modena and Pisa, whilst the Guelfs are strongest in Bologna, Genoa, and Mantua. Most other places are flexible, even opportunistic, in their allegiances.

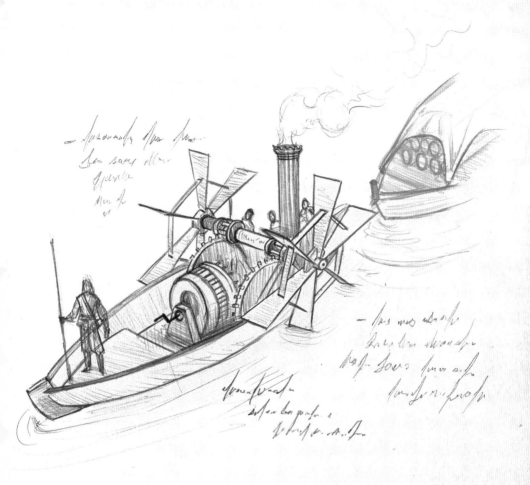

Despite the Papal State's distaste for these 'devil's pack-mules', one modern
steam-powered fiumicular – the Saint Christopher – plies the mighty Tiber River,
bringing Rome cheap wine and olive oil from Perugia and timber from Umbria.

EUROPE

The paradox is that although most people live, labour, marry, and die within a couple of days' walk of where they were born at most, this is an era of growing mobility, as merchants, scholars, soldiers, explorers, and diplomats roam further and further, connecting Italy to the rest of Europe and the lands beyond.

FRANCE

One of the great powers of the age, France casts a shadow over the Italian peninsula. Milan is in its grip and its armies, with their fearsome Compagnies d'Ordnance and mighty cannon, have marched all the way down the peninsula to Naples and periodically go to war with Venice. To King Louis XII, Italy matters less than France's perennial rivals – Spain, England, and the Holy Roman Empire – but it remains to be seen whether Florence's rise will alter that opinion.

Whilst France is the most populous country in Europe, its people are nonetheless fragmented amongst local identities and dominions – most would consider themselves Orléanais, Parisian, or something else first, and French second. The French Church also possesses vast riches, which means monarchs are often eager to assert their own authority over it, much to the fury of the Vatican. There is still more than enough left over, however, for royal wars, noble self-indulgence, and a growing artistic and scholarly culture in France's cities. For the Italians, France, compared with backward Spain and the dour Holy Roman Empire, is still often where they look for inspiration.

Guide's Notes

France in *Gran Meccanismo* is at once a distant land of glittering palaces and huge cities (Paris is one and a half times as big as Milan or Venice) and a very immediate player in Italian politics, threatening the independence of the city states. If anything, its military successes have led people to overestimate its interest and capacity, but it is still powerful, cultured, arrogant, and ambitious.

SPAIN

The Kingdoms of Castile and Aragon were recently united with the marriage of Ferdinand II of Aragon and Isabella I of Castile and, although Isabella died in 1504, Ferdinand remains the effective monarch of all Spain (except the Basque lands, which are next on his list). Spain is rich and powerful – and hopes to become much more so now that it has begun to explore the New World – but also generally considered backward in its ways, in the iron grip of the most hard-line Catholicism and an effete aristocracy. In 1492, the Edict of Expulsion forced all Jews to convert to Christianity or leave Spain, and many fled to Italy. Muslims are now facing the same fate. As a result, although it may be a caricature, educated Italians consider Spain, in the words of one pamphleteer, 'an idiot giant'.

Guide's Notes

Spain matters because of its rule over the Italian south and its status as a counterweight to France, but it feels rather more distant in the Italy of *Gran Meccanismo*, in part because its eyes are directed towards the New World (and its old rival, England), and in part because, unlike France, it does not have the same cultural capital. Unless you are a Church fundamentalist, Spain is a land with which you may want to trade, or even form an alliance, but it is not one that you want to copy.

ENGLAND

The energetic, ambitious, and over-sexed King Henry VIII has just ascended to the English throne, bringing with him an assertive foreign policy. In practice, this will mean war, especially as he has his eye on a reconquest of France. England is far away, but the entrepreneurialism of the English and Italian bankers and merchants means there are many connections, with English mercenaries serving in Italy's wars, Italian bankers offering credit in London, and a healthy trade in wool and weapons between the two – ideas and influence are heading both ways.

Guide's Notes

England is unlikely to play a direct role in the Italy of *Gran Meccanismo*, but its status as a more than faintly piratical geopolitical player may mean it crops up, whether as a foil against France or Spain or because Henry – always fascinated by the latest fads – becomes interested in the New Science.

THE HOLY ROMAN EMPIRE

From the borders of France in the west to Poland in the east stretches the Holy Roman Empire, a Germanic political bloc of kingdoms, duchies, and protectorates, all subordinated to Emperor Maximilian of the House of Habsburg. Technically, he is also King of the Romans, although his real authority in Italy is limited, which is one of the reasons he has become embroiled in wars in the north of the country – not least to prevent French expansion. In 1508, Pope Julius II brought Maximilian together with France's Louis XII and Spain's Ferdinand II in the League of Cambrai to break Venice, and whilst this alliance was initially successful, it has just fallen apart because of Vatican suspicions about Paris. Julius II is now seeking to find a common cause with Venice against France, and Maximilian may smile on this endeavour. After all, to him, France is the real rival for power in Europe, with Italy as just another theatre for this conflict. However, his foreign adventures are costing the Empire dearly, and the assorted dukes, princes, and free cities of the Holy Roman Empire are becoming increasingly restive. For as long as he can keep them under control, though, Maximilian has formidable military, political, and economic power at his disposal.

Guide's Notes

The Holy Roman Empire is another foreign power treating Italy as both a potential trophy and a place for proxy wars. Although only the lands around Verona are currently controlled by the Empire, a relic of the League of Cambrai's wars against Venice, this could change quickly. Should characters venture into the Empire, though, they will find it a very varied and different setting, with medieval petty baronies next to rapidly expanding modern Germanic cities such as Vienna, the seat of Habsburg power.

MALTA AND THE ORDER OF ST JOHN

Valletta, on the island of Malta, rules the rest of its small archipelago to the south of Sicily, of which only the other two larger islands – Gozo and Comino – are inhabited. However, all three tend to be lumped together as 'Malta'. With a coastline crinkled with numerous natural bays, and situated at the crossroads of Mediterranean trade, it has time and again been conquered by imperial powers who see it as a valuable trading and raiding base – the Phoenicians, the Romans, the Arabs, and then the Normans of the Kingdom of Sicily in 1091. Today, it remains a territory of Sicily, in turn a dependency of Spain. However, this year the rising Ottoman Empire pushed the crusading Order of Knights of the Hospital of St John of Jerusalem, commonly known as the Knights Hospitaller, out of their last stronghold on the Greek island of Rhodes. The Spanish crown, looking to protect a bulwark against the Turks, offered them Malta as a new base, along with Gozo and the port city of Tripoli on the North African coast – all for the annual fee of a single Maltese falcon presented to the Viceroy of Sicily every All Souls' Day and the promise to defend Rome against Islam.

Crusader knights from the Order's scattered commanderies are arriving from the east, shifting power to the coastal town of Birgu. There, Grand Master Philippe Villiers de L'Isle-Adam has decided their base will be Fort St Angelo, a bastioned fortress at the heart of Birgu's Grand Harbour, currently in ruins but being rebuilt at speed. The aim is to make it as impregnable a fortress as possible, and it is rumoured that de L'Isle-Adam is even toying with adopting New Science weapons, feeling that the need to defend the Order's new home permits perhaps some 'creativity' with the Papal ban on them. That may well lead him into conflict with Pope Julius II, but that will be another day.

Malta is poor, and the Order has lost much. If the Order is to fortify the island as it wants, it needs to spend much, too. The Order is gathering its fleet behind de L'Isle-Adam's flagship the *Santa Anna* and is planning to become something of a Mediterranean police force, taking on the Barbary pirates from North Africa who regularly raid the shipping of the western Mediterranean with the blessing of the Ottomans. Christian shipping will be protected and Christian slaves freed – and pirate ships and cargoes will be seized and sold for the good of the Order's coffers.

Guide's Notes

The Order is something between a medieval Mediterranean police force, an army of crusading zealots, and a multi-national mercenary business. Malta itself is a bustling place undergoing significant reconstruction, its old, comfortable ways upended as the battle-scarred, militant knights of the Order bring their own rules and lifestyle.

ORUÇ REIS, 'BARBAROSSA', BADASS OTTOMAN PIRATE

The son of a minor Ottoman official, Oruç Reis turned out to be born for a life on the sea. A naval commander and pirate chieftain – the two are pretty interchangeable when it comes to the struggles between the Ottomans and Christendom in the Mediterranean – he has harried Knights Hospitaller shipping out of Rhodes, captured galleons off the coast of Naples, and taken Papal galleys leaving Elba. At his base on the Tunisian island of Djerba, he has assembled a fleet, attracted to his command by his daring and his seamanship. He also worked unstintingly to evacuate Muslims expelled from Spain, who called him Baba Oruç (Father Oruç). This sounded enough like Barbarossa (Redbeard) to Italian ears to give him his European nickname. Merry, ruthless, adventurous, and even chivalrous, he is the toast of the Ottoman court – and a terror to European shipping.

Body 4, Mind 3, Soul 5. Ottoman Through and Through 5d, Pirate Chieftain 8d, Daring Seamanship 7d, Swashbuckler 6d, Remember My Name 5d

FURTHER AFIELD

THE OTTOMAN EMPIRE

The mighty Ottoman Empire is on the rise and on the march. Mehmed the Conqueror took Constantinople in 1453, and his successor, Bayezid II, is proving just as effective a statesman. His elite soldiers, the Janissaries, have pushed Venice out of its Greek territories and crushed rebellions in Anatolia and beyond, whilst at sea Ottoman raiders roam the Mediterranean, seizing Christian ships and enslaving their crews. Yet Bayezid II is also a wise and cultured ruler, known by the epithet 'the Just'. He has welcomed Jews expelled from Spain, and his court is renowned for its elegance and learning. In 1509, however, Constantinople was rocked by a terrible earthquake, and Bayezid's sons Selim and Ahmet have begun vying for the succession, raising the prospect of civil strife and even civil war. Meanwhile, the Ottomans are heirs to a centuries-long tradition of science and experimentation in the Arab world, and as the New Science rises, it is rumoured that they are rediscovering the work of pioneers such as Hasan al-Rammah, the thirteenth-century Syrian who studied the secrets of gunpowder.

Guide's Notes

The other major powers are all European and Christian, whilst the Ottomans are indisputably 'other'. For some, this will mean that they are enemies by definition, but for others, it makes them less of a threat, as they have other concerns, and they are treated with a degree of respect (one can feel more bitter about a feud with a neighbour or a cousin than with some distant party). Adventuring in Ottoman lands in *Gran Meccanismo* would be an interestingly different experience; it's worth remembering that the Ottomans are much more tolerant of other faiths and peoples than the Europeans. The open question is whether the Ottomans seriously begin to develop their own version of the New Science, and whether this extends to active espionage in Italy or attempts to woo thinkers and adventurers.

MUSCOVY

Ironically, Muscovy feels, to most Europeans, more alien and distant than the Ottoman Empire. Grand Prince Vasily III continues his dynasty's campaign to assert control over all the scattered principalities of the Rus'. One day he may turn his eyes to Eastern Europe, and even the lands to the south, but today is not that day. Nonetheless, there are trade links, and Italian artists and architects increasingly find themselves offered lucrative opportunities to make the long journey to bring their ideas to the Grand Prince's court. Indeed, the new fortress, the Kremlin, built in Moscow, is very similar to the Sforza Castle in Milan, designed and built by a slew of Italian architects.

Guide's Notes

Very much an outlier in the world of *Gran Meccanismo*, Muscovy nonetheless does have its place, precisely because it is increasingly looking to Italy as the place to shop for ideas and designs. Pragmatic, willing to assimilate ideas from wherever they find them, and acutely aware of their technological weaknesses, the Muscovites might look to the New Science as a way of accelerating their efforts to unify the Russians under their rule, as well as potentially leapfrogging their rivals in Poland and the Baltic.

AFRICA

There are two Africas in the mind of most Italians. North Africa is largely Muslim territory, the lands of the Hafsid Caliphate and the Kingdom of Tlemcen, but above all, known and feared for the Barbary pirates. They raid not just across the breadth of the Mediterranean but even as far north as Scandinavia, their prisoners ending up sold as slaves in Constantinople and the Levant. Beyond that are lands scarcely known to the Italians, even though Africans are an increasing, if still rare, sight in Italy since the Papal Bulls (decrees) of the mid-fifteenth century outlawed the old practices of slavery. However, Spain and Portugal remain hubs for African slave-trading and, now that expelled Jews are finding new homes in Italy, some communities of Africans in Italy, supported by progressive circles, are looking for ways to smuggle escaped slaves there, too. Meanwhile, Emperor Dawid II of Ethiopia has begun sending emissaries to European courts, seeking allies against the Ottoman-backed Muslim states around his Christian realm. With Spain, Portugal, and France yet to respond, might he try reaching out to Venice, Rome, or even Florence?

Guide's Notes

Africans are a rare but not unknown sight in the Italy of *Gran Meccanismo*. They will include traders, political refugees, escaped slaves, artisans, and a growing number of second- or third-generation Italians who, especially in the more liberal northern territories, are also emerging as scholars and artists. Most of Africa itself, though, is still very much *terra incognita*.

Niccolò Machiavelli, Florence's State Secretary and Commissioner for Peace and War, is an afficionado of the new-fangled game of chess, but his mind is not on the game. The Pope wants Florence to burn. The French are jealous of the city's New Science. Da Vinci and Soderini, the city's greatest mind and its most powerful politician respectively, are increasingly seduced by the thought that human imperfection can be 'solved' by hydronetic computation. And, tonight, the in-laws are coming to dinner.

FLORENCE

With its red roofs and white-plastered buildings, and a skyline studded with the spires of churches and the broad dome of the Duomo, Florence is a beautiful city – and it knows it. Its location on the Arno River means that it has long been an important centre for trade and commerce, first as the hub of the European wool industry, and later for the emerging new business of banking. Woolpacks from England, spices from the east, businessmen looking for credit, diplomats seeking a neutral place to meet, students, scholars, entrepreneurs, and opportunists are all a common sight in Florence. The city has become rich and this, along with influences and ideas from all the known world, has generated a unique cultural fermentation.

From the fourteenth century, Florence – Firenze – was dominated by the Medici family, whose wealth came from banking and whose power came from investing their massive fortunes into everything from mercenary armies to political favours. Patrons of the arts and learning, their star rose steadily, and Florence's with it. The city state was technically a republic but, in practice, the Medici were largely able to get their way – through patronage, influence, or, when necessary, muscle. The high water mark of their power was the time of Lorenzo de'Medici, known as Lorenzo the Magnificent. A statesman, patron of the arts, and canny ruler, he was able to maintain stability across Italy, albeit at the cost of angering the ambitious Pope Sixtus IV, who even tried to have him assassinated.

When Lorenzo died in 1492, the old order began to fall apart – his son was not known as Piero the Unfortunate without reason. When King Charles VIII of France invaded Italy in 1494, heading for Naples, Piero first tried to face him down, then gave in to his every demand, including handing over the towns of Pisa and Livorno. A furious Florentine mob drove him into exile, re-establishing a republican government. Probably, the fiery Dominican monk Girolamo Savonarola, with his radical views about church reform and the coming of the End of Days, would have become the dominant force, had he not recently died of what looked like a seizure but was rumoured to have been a secret assassination.

NICCOLÒ MACHIAVELLI

Scholar, diplomat, philosopher, and bureaucrat, Machiavelli has long been a student of statecraft, and now he has a unique opportunity to put his knowledge into practice. By any reckoning, he has been extraordinarily successful, but he is also smart enough to know that fate can quickly turn against those it has favoured, and he is beginning to grow concerned that the New Science that has been such a boon could also be a bane, whether it attracts conquerors from France, the Holy Roman Empire, or the Vatican, or it replaces human agency altogether with dispassionate hydronetics. After all, Machiavelli's weakness is, that for all he understands power, he cannot help but balance it with virtue. What is the virtuous prince to do next?

Body 2, Mind 6, Soul 3. Clear-sighted Manager 10d, Master of Manipulation 7d, Just as I Predicted 6d, Secret Worrier 5d

THE SIGNORIA AND
THE BUREAUCRACY

What became known as the Great November Revolution of 1494 thus ended up transferring power down a rung, from the Medici to the officials, lesser aristocrats, and merchant bankers who had done the real work of government for them. In theory, rule rests with the Signoria (Lordship), a council of nine. Eight of them are the Priors, chosen by lot to serve two-month terms, six of whom come from the major guilds, two from the minor ones. The ninth is the Gonfaloniere (Standard-bearer), the commander-in-chief of the republic's military and effectively its president.

The Priors get to stay in the Palazzo della Signoria, wear smart red coats trimmed with ermine, and are paid a stipend, but their actual role is little more than ceremonial. Much the same is true of the two lesser councils: the Twelve Good Men, three elected from each of the city's four neighbourhoods, and the Sixteen Standard-bearers, speaking for its military companies. Real power rests instead in the bureaucracy, especially in three overlapping committees: the Ten of War (who handle military affairs), the Eight of Security (domestic policy), and the Six of Commerce (trade and finance).

In 1502, Piero Soderini was elected – by the people who mattered – to be Gonfaloniere for life. It was a good choice: he has shown himself sensible, moderate, a fine broker of consensus and resolver of disputes. He was also clever enough to put his trust, and a great deal of power, in the hands of men smarter and more driven than he. In particular, this means Niccolò Machiavelli, his clear-sighted and cool-headed secretary (which, in practice, means deputy), who manages to chair both the Ten of War and the Eight of Security, as well as being one of the Six of Commerce. He has been a prime mover behind the adoption of the New Science, but he is by no means the only extraordinary figure in these extraordinary times.

It is important to remember that Florence's new rulers are, in their own ways, revolutionaries. They are, in the main, smart, ambitious, opportunistic, and educated, steeped as much in the arts as the sciences, as much in humanistic philosophy as religious teaching. But they had all been outsiders, seemingly locked out of power by the hereditary rule of the Medici and a handful of other oligarch families. Suddenly given their own chance to rule, they want to change the world.

THE NEW SCIENCE

This is the time of the New Science. It was Machiavelli who saw the potential in the tortured genius of Leonardo da Vinci. Da Vinci had been employed by Milan's Ludovico Sforza until the French supplanted him, whereupon he fled to Venice, which returned him to his home city of Florence in 1500. He set up shop as an artist, but Machiavelli happened to glance at some of his fanciful designs and saw in them not just the republic's survival, but its future.

When, at last, a patron with the necessary will and resources wanted to support da Vinci the inventor rather than da Vinci the artist, the result was an explosion of creativity. Furthermore, to everyone's surprise, most of these inventions actually worked – excluding the odd teething problem, false start, and, in one particularly memorable case, a percussive explosion that blew half a palazzo into the Arno River and blinded da Vinci in one eye. Mathematicians and natural scientists claim that there is no way his gliders should be able to lift a man or that the water-powered cogent engines should work. And yet they do.

What da Vinci started, many others have continued and developed in all kinds of new directions. For example, Gianpiero Tartaglia is turning out to be a master mechanician, whose automata began as fanciful props for plays and parties but are now becoming fashionable guardians and household servants. Isabella Cortese, once dismissed as an 'alchemist', is now creating a new body of knowledge in the practical codification of chemistry. The astronomer Camillo Leonardi is using the new optical magnoscope invented by Renzo Ciano to scan the skies, and dreams of one day building a glider that is able to fly to the moon. More pragmatically, if you want a flintlock gun that can fit into a bracelet or a lock that spits Greek fire if anyone tries to pick it, then the one-eyed ex-condotierre Manfredo Manfredi is your man.

This technological revolution has also led to extraordinary social change. Old prejudices against women, Jews, and others seem to have been swept away in the rush to find the most imaginative inventors, the most precise crafters, and the sharpest mathematicians. The so-called clockers, the hydronetic engineers and programmers of the cogent engines, have become a subculture of their own, whilst a new generation of military engineers is calling for war simply for a chance to test their new infernal devices. No wonder the Pope damns the New Science in increasingly sulphurous sermons, as even some members of the clergy have begun to claim that the path to God can be found not in scripture and Church dogma but in numbers and the pursuit of the natural sciences.

Da Vinci himself, working with his friend, the brilliant mathematician and Franciscan friar Luca de Pacioli, has become more and more consumed, perhaps to the point of obsession, with hydronetics – the workings of the new cogent engines – and especially with the increasingly massive and capable Gran Meccanismo (Great Mechanism). Having once sought to understand the workings of the human body by dissecting cadavers, tracing tendons and duplicating joints, now he seems to think that one can understand, and even perfect, the workings of human society by modelling it through brass cogwheels, dripping reservoirs, and pasteboard punch-cards. Some think this impossible – but, then again, they said the same about manned flight, and one need only glance towards the sky on a clear day to see who was correct on that count.

People say the New Science got under Leonardo da Vinci's skin, and into his soul. That childlike curiosity about everything around him has sharpened into an obsessive need to understand, code, and maybe even control all the vagaries of the world. Even the accident that burned out his eye will not stop him.

THE GRAN MECCANISMO

Bit by bit, an early experiment into logical processes turned into a simple calculating engine powered by a water clock, roughly the size of a workbench. From there, the machine eventually became increasingly complex, thanks to the genius of both de Pacioli and the Arab astronomer Abu Ishaq al-Juzjani, becoming able to resolve in minutes mathematical and logical problems that would occupy a human brain for weeks. And so it expanded, bit by bit, often in a haphazard and unplanned way, until today it occupies not just the Palazzo Altoviti in the heart of Florence, backing onto the river by the Holy Trinity Bridge, but also the deep cellars dug out below. Waterwheels along the Arno, a windmill on the roof, and three great capstans in the courtyard next door, turned day and night by prisoners of war and debtors, all power its grinding gears, whirring flywheels, and click-clacking logic gates.

The Gran Meccanismo is increasingly important in the governance of Florence and at the heart of a growing debate about the future. Its weather forecasts are invaluable to Florence's farmers, sailors, and glider pilots alike. Architects and bankers book time with one of its computational clerks to crunch load ratios and annual accounts. The Catalogo identity card all Florentine citizens now must carry is punched to allow it to be checked against the records in the Gran Meccanismo, or the smaller terminals – the Repeaters – at city gates and main government buildings, each of which is issued with an updated drum of records by an armed squad of the Signoria's Guard every dawn.

And here's where things begin to get heated. Is this a step towards tyranny? So far, it is rare for anyone to have to show their card, but that could change, and already some are burning them in protest. The threat is that they will deprive themselves of the right to vote, or of the tax breaks due to all full citizens of Florence. Some claim that decisions about everything, from what to spend on the city's defences to when to schedule festivals, are being made by the Gran Meccanismo, as Soderini succumbs to the new fad for metrics and 'hydronetic management'. Even more sinister are the suggestions that the rotary dials and clockwork printers it uses to show its results have begun spooling out unprompted observations, and that its great logic drums have been heard turning and chittering on their own at night.

Guide's Notes

You get to decide just what the Gran Meccanismo is. Is it a weird piece of background science, a weapon at Florence's disposal, a secret weakness that will lead to disaster as people depend too much on it, or a virtual intelligence on the brink of becoming self-aware? It could be any of these things.

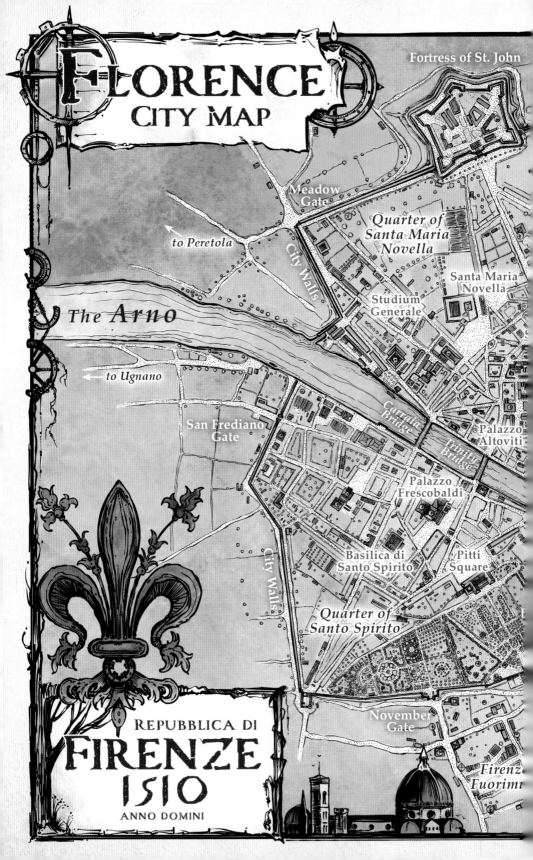

FLORENCE
CITY MAP

Fortress of St. John

Meadow Gate

Quarter of Santa Maria Novella

to Peretola

City Walls

Santa Maria Novella

Studium Generale

The *Arno*

to Ugnano

Carraia Bridge

Palazzo Altoviti

Trinity Bridge

San Frediano Gate

Palazzo Frescobaldi

Basilica di Santo Spirito

Pitti Square

City Walls

Quarter of Santo Spirito

November Gate

Firenz Fuorim

REPUBBLICA DI
FIRENZE
1510
ANNO DOMINI

Cockerel Gate

to Fiesole

Quarter of
San Giovanni

City Walls

Pinti
Gate

Mattonaia

Santa Maria
dei Fiori

New Hospital
of St. Mary

Cross
Gate

gello

Shinbone

Quarter of
Santa Croce

azzo
chio

Basilica of
Santa Croce

Bridge of
the Graces

The *Arno*

Aliantodrome

Il Camino

igli

o Arcetri

FLORENCE
QUARTER BY QUARTER

The walled city itself is divided into four *quartieri* (quarters), each named after the most important church it holds and each with its own character, council and heraldry. Many Florentines feel a deep loyalty to their quarter, especially in the regular football matches that take place between their teams in the main squares – events for which baying mobs turn out, wearing their quarter's colours.

Three of the quarters fan out across the northern bank of the Arno River, roughly along the line of the great stone bridge of the Ponte alla Carraia. To the north west is the **Quarter of Santa Maria Novella**, named after the great marble-facaded **Church of Santa Maria Novella**, said to be a haven still for Papal loyalists who merely affect loyalty to the Signoria whilst smuggling reports back to Rome. The **Palazzo Altoviti**, home of the Gran Meccanismo, is the focus of continuing and controversial construction, with new waterwheels being built to meet its ever-growing demand for power. The main building of the **Studium Generale**, Florence's university, is also here, although in practice many scholars simply teach out of their homes or in a nearby square or garden.

The most impressive church in the northern **Quarter of San Giovanni** is the mighty **Santa Maria del Fiore** cathedral, the Duomo, pride of the city, which stands next to the Baptistery of San Giovanni that gives the quarter its name. The **Fortress of St John the Baptist** is a craggy medieval stronghold, updated for the gunpowder era with V-shaped bastions, now studded with cannon and new steam-powered crossbows. This fortress not only holds the barracks of the Signoria's Guard but also is where the city's turtle-tanks are housed and maintained. The bastions on each side of the **Cockerel Gate** are likewise new, with organ guns mounted to deliver a withering crossfire to any who seek to storm it.

To the north east, the **Quarter of Santa Croce** (Holy Cross) takes its name from the great Dominican cathedral. In the square in front of the church, a city-wide football tournament is held once every year, and the rest of the time, mechanici have taken to displaying designs and models of their inventions, hoping to attract buyers and patrons (whilst trying to sneak a surreptitious glance at their rivals' wares). To the east of the quarter, around the Piazza della Signoria, is the **Palazzo della Signoria**, also called the **Palazzo Vecchio** (Old Palace), the tall, fortified centre of Florence's government. The equally fortified **Bargello** is the headquarters for Florence's police, commanded by the official also known as the Bargello. Nearby is the notorious **Shinbone,** Florence's main prison. Once a place for debtors, drunks, and blasphemers, this moated fortress is increasingly filling up with political prisoners as the republic's leadership more vigorously cracks down on dissent, or, depending on whom you believe, simply is able to track its enemies more efficiently. Those with money can rent better rooms and buy decent food, but for the rest it is a place of dark, damp cells and little hope of escape. The **New Hospital of St Mary** is one of the city's oldest, but is generally considered its best. The new bastion to the east of the city, guarding a potentially vulnerable spot on the outer walls, was built with fine red brick, and is thus called the **Mattonaia**, 'the Brickyard'.

The medieval **Ponte Vecchio** (Old Bridge) is just one of many across the Arno, but the shops built along its span are now known for selling the products of the city's alchemists, from cosmetics to sovereign tonics that cure whatever ails you. It connects Santa Croce with the **Quarter of Santo Spirito**, also known as **Oltrarno**, (Over the Arno). It is largely a working-class neighbourhood, although the new, rich mercantile classes are beginning to buy up ramshackle old housing to demolish and build themselves new palaces. This has contributed to some ugly riots, and the **Palazzo Frescobaldi** now houses a permanent garrison of militiamen just in case, as does **Fort Belvedere** on a low hill along the outer walls, but **Pitti Square** has nonetheless become a place for frequent demonstrations and protests. When the Medici fell from power, the Signoria confiscated part of their lands inside the walls, and the new **November Quarter**, inside the equally-new **November Gate** – both named for the 1494 Revolution – is a neighbourhood of hurriedly built standardised social housing, identical streets distinguished only by number and colour in a pattern deemed most efficient by the Gran Meccanismo.

The city has inevitably expanded beyond its fourteenth-century walls, especially in its current economic boom. **Firenze Fuorimuri** (Florence Outside the Walls) is an unplanned mix of slums and social housing, as well as workshops and warehouses that have sprung up around the newly built labour prison of **Le Gigli**. Here, Commissioner for Restorative Labour Oreste Burrone, one of the government's most enthusiastic advocates of hydronetic management, oversees an experiment in 'freedom through labour'. Instead of simply sitting in their cells, those convicted of the most serious crimes, from murder to sedition, work from dawn to dusk, not least on winding machines, coiling springs to power all kinds of New Science inventions. Every year, on the feast day of St Leonard, patron saint of prisoners, Le Gigli puts on a display of carefully drilled enthusiasm as the convicts praise the regime in which they work and enjoy their rare day off. Closer to the walls is the open space and distinctive barn-hangars of the **Aliantodrome**, the city's gliderport. The tall new watchtower known as **Il Camino** (the Chimney), guards the approaches – and keeps a wary eye on the neighbourhood's unruly mix of migrants, paupers, fugitives, and indigents.

Further out are villages and neighbourhoods that are slowly being incorporated into the city as it creeps ever outwards. To the west are the state farms of **Peretola**, worked by republican farmers, debtors, and prisoners of war, and beyond them is **Ugnano**, a village now being converted into the Polygon – a huge military base with barracks for the Urban Militia and workshops to house and maintain some of the new weapons at their disposal. On the hills above the city, **Fiesole** is a fashionable town where the rich retire to their mansions in summer, but is now also, thanks to its altitude, the home of the School of the Air, where glider pilots are trained. The Gallo Tower in the hilltop village of **Arcetri** is part of the city's outer defences, now equipped with a signal-fire and semaphores to signal sight of invaders.

EVERYDAY LIFE

Whilst in the towns the routine may vary slightly, in the countryside, from dawn to dusk, the peasantry labour in their fields and farmhouses – a hard life, but one in which they find their joys where they can. Peasants might eat fish if they live near the coast, or otherwise a little meat on rare occasion, but in the main they live off pasta, polenta, grains, bread, some cheese, and soup made of, well, whatever they can find to put in it. In the towns, meals is much the same, although discarded food from wealthier citizens adds to the variety of the diet.

Life is marked and enlivened by church days, religious festivals, and civic celebrations, often accompanied by riotous traditions and hand-outs of food and drink as the rich and powerful try to outdo each other with displays of civic-minded altruism (or, more cynically, try to win over the mob). These traditions often involve physicality to the point of outright violence, and they are an excuse to subvert the social order and to mock the Church and the aristocracy, who put up with it because it's just for a day and it's better than a revolution.

Every city has its own distinctive festivals. In Florence, for example, Easter Sunday is marked by the Bursting of the Wagon. A cart bearing a tower of fireworks is pulled by two white oxen, bedecked in flowers, through the city to the square in front of the Duomo, escorted by a guard of honour and the Standard-bearers of all the districts of the city. From the altar, the archbishop lights the touchpaper and fireworks propel a symbolic 'dove' along a wire stretched the length of the cathedral to set off the wagon.

Whilst the people's faith is often as much as about ritual, superstition, and such displays as it is about God, it is nonetheless real, and even the most ardent apostles of the New Science think they are simply learning new ways to understand God's universe rather than challenging the existence of the divine. However, they also join a growing chorus of thinkers who doubt that the Vatican can still be considered the infallible interpreter of divine will.

In the cities, a new middle class is beginning to emerge from the more successful artisans, artists, clerks, merchants, priests, and lawyers. Some live almost as hand-to-mouth an existence as the poor, but others are rising as power starts to shift from the landed warrior aristocracy to the new oligarchs of banking and politics. However, for the moment, they all coexist and, indeed, intermarry, as bankers forge alliances with grand old families for the prestige, whilst they mend the aristocracy's threadbare fortunes as their part of the deal.

Despite occasional bouts of sumptuary laws – which limit displays of extravagance because the Church considers them an expression of sinful pride and secular rulers are trying to prevent aristocrats spending themselves into debt – on the whole this is an age when if you have it, you flaunt it. Even the poor will pull out a brightly-coloured shawl they inherited from their grandmother or a handmade half-cloak when it is a feast day. For those of greater means, money is freely spent on hiring the services of famous artists and architects, holding extravagant banquets, and buying the most exquisite jewellery. Even when you die, money you had set aside is used to build a grandiose tomb of the finest Carrara marble and pay a church to pray for your soul every year.

MEN AND WOMEN

Medieval notions of a man's and a woman's roles are just beginning to be questioned and subverted, although in the main the assumption is that a woman's primary function is to be a wife and mother, and, in the case of the aristocracy, married off for the good of the dynasty. But even in this age of dowries, family alliances, and ruthless pragmatism, there is still a role for love and respect within marriage.

However, the times – especially with the accelerating social change generated first by the Renaissance and then by the New Science – are seeing steadily greater options for women looking beyond their traditional roles. Women have begun to emerge as scholars, authors, inventors, and even rulers in their own right. Isabella d'Este is not only proving to be an able and cunning regent in Mantua, but she is also at the heart of a web of correspondents, especially of educated women, across Italy. Felice della Rovere, illegitimate daughter of Pope Julius II, is an accomplished businesswoman in her own right. Vittoria Colonna, marchioness of Pescara, is fast becoming one of the most popular poets in Italy.

Nor is this purely confined to the aristocracy. Some of the brightest clockers exploring the potential of hydronetics and the new cogent engines are women, as are a growing number of bankers, especially in the smaller, more risk-taking family banks. There are female traders, scholars, and even some fighters, although war is still largely the province of men. Many convents are involved in business, from beekeeping and brewing to making cosmetics and offering letter-writing services, and with this many nuns are finding it possible to reconcile God and trade.

Of course, none of this is easy, and women still face all kinds of burdens and prejudices – especially in the countryside and in the south – but as with so many old attitudes, change is coming.

CLOCKERS

'Clocker' is the term for anyone who specialises in programming or using cogent engines, from the computational clerks in the Palazzo Altoviti and the operators manning the Repeaters to the builders experimenting with their own designs and punch-card programmes. However, in practice, it tends to be primarily used for those who are outside the mainstream – the young devotees of hydronetics putting in all-nighters, convinced they are about to create a better water-clock processor; the freelance programmers; and, especially, those who would intrude into the workings of the cogent engines, from the simple machines running automated looms and metal-presses to the Gran Meccanismo itself, to access information or even change their programmes. With their scruffy multi-pocket vests (to carry blank cards, a hole punch, clockdrives, and the other tools of their trade), and their talk of 'waterware', 'spindrives', 'overclocking', and 'drips' (the basic unit of memory), they represent a new youth subculture in Florence, regarded with suspicion, enthusiasm, or incomprehension.

BUSINESS

Out in the countryside, barter is still the order of the day – and even in the poorer quarters of the cities, goods and services are more often swapped or owed than paid for with cash. Those who do use money must consider the bewildering array of coins in circulation. The gold florin minted in Florence would be worth, in modern money, anything up to £700 ($1000), and was equivalent to 7 silver lire (a pound of silver), or around 140 silver soldi, or something like a thousand copper denari. But other cities mint their own florins, often of different weights and purity of gold, as do other countries. How many German rheingulden for a Venetian ducat? Transactions involving more than the smallest coins or florins get incredibly complex, as exchange rates vary by the day, which is why banking has become an increasingly complex art (and why *Gran Meccanismo* keeps financial matters abstract!).

BANKING AND CREDIT

Where does the word 'bank' come from? The answer is the *banco*, a plain wooden counter covered in a green cloth that bankers would set out in markets and other suitable locations from which to conduct their business. Until the thirteenth century, banking was solely the purview of Jews, because the Church forbade usury – lending money for interest – but, as everyone needed to borrow money at some time or other, eventually Christians found ways around the ban. The first were the Bardi and Peruzzi families of Florence, who realised that, even if you technically don't charge interest, you can still make money from loans by charging fees. They later went bankrupt, learning a bitter lesson that lending to kings can be dangerous when you have no way of forcing them to pay back their loan.

Since then, other great families and commercial combines have moved into the business, especially the mighty Medici (who set up their bank in 1397). However, Jews are still powerful players in the field, especially because they are also dominant in the pawnbroking industry – the lending of small sums in return for handing over tools, clothes, jewellery, and the like as collateral. This is an essential service for many, and the spectacle of an artisan with pretentions pawning his best coat every Monday, only to redeem it for church on Sunday, is not at all uncommon.

There are now some 80 banks in Florence alone, from great financial enterprises like the Gondi Bank and the Monte di Pietà to little solo outfits and branches of banks based elsewhere, including the Fuggers of Bavaria and the Monte dei Paschi of Siena. As well as deposits, loans, and money-changing, they provide the new-fangled 'letters of credit' that allow merchants to travel without vulnerable chests full of cash. The banker signs the document, committing the bank to pay a certain sum to the bearer as part of a transaction and, when the seller presents proof that they has completed their side of the bargain to the buyer's satisfaction, the bank pays out the agreed sum.

This has revolutionised trade and banking, but also puts a premium on the banker being sure that he or she isn't being fleeced. As banks become bigger and their activities more complex, they also become more and more dependent on the quality of the information at their disposal. Whose business is about to go bust? Which city is about to debase its currency, making its coins a little smaller or mixing copper in with the silver or gold? Who is a drunk and a gambler, likely to fritter away any loans with no collateral left to be seized? It would be not too far-fetched to suggest that the large banks are also private intelligence agencies in their own right.

FINANCIAL CRIME

The rise of banks, letters of credit, and the rest of this new financial system has brought with it new kinds of crime. For as long as there has been money, there have been frauds, counterfeiters, and coin shavers (who pare away the edges of coins, slowly accumulating enough precious metal to mint their own coin). The Renaissance is having to come to terms with insurance fraud, forged letters of credit, pyramid financial schemes (which seem to offer wonderful returns until they go bust), and tax evasion. A cynic would say this last, at least, is the norm – most merchants keep formal accounts to show the tax assessor and a *libro segreto* (secret book) with the real figures.

WAR

This is a time of conflict, when the city states of the Italian peninsula routinely make war upon each other. Everyone remembers the French invasion of 1494, when a mighty foreign army sliced right the way down through Italy, for a while taking Florence and Rome on its way to Naples. It took the Holy League, an alliance of Rome, Milan, Venice, Spain, and the Holy Roman Empire, to drive them out. Warfare is only just adapting to the gunpowder era, and the spear, sword, crossbow, and pike are still dominant, even though firearms and cannon are increasingly common and already making heavy metal armour obsolete.

CONDOTTIERI AND MILITIAS

Most Italian city states still rely on hiring mercenaries. States engage mercenary commanders, known as *condottieri* (contractors) to raise private armies, whether for invasion or defence. Some of these condottieri are cunning tacticians and inspirational leaders, but most are first and foremost entrepreneurs. Their armies are their businesses and so they do whatever they can to prolong lucrative wars and avoid casualties. In the past, wars have often been lengthy games of feint and manoeuvre, until one side finds itself in an untenable position, at which point, perhaps after a face-saving skirmish or two, it sues for peace.

Two schools of military thought dominate condottieri operations, each named for their early fifteenth-century originators and masters: Muzio Attendolo – who became known as Sforza – and Braccio da Montone. Sforza was a master of preparation, concentrating combined infantry and cavalry forces so as to have local dominance, and then unleashing a carefully planned and coordinated hammer blow. Conversely, Bracceschi tactics depend on speed and precision, with multiple cavalry squadrons under tight control finding and exploiting the enemy's vulnerabilities before throwing in the reserve force to break them.

However, Machiavelli soon realised the flaws in this model, especially as relying on mercenaries brought the danger that they would turn against you or demand more money. Instead, he envisaged Florence guarded by a militia of its own citizens, professionally trained, disciplined, devoted to their city, and commanded by soldiers who owed their rank to ability, not birth. It took three years of lobbying and politicking, but in 1506, he was finally able to form this new model army, and to arm them with the fruits of the New Science.

This is probably just as well, because the French invasions also demonstrated that the relatively small armies of Italy, combined with the condottieri's dislike of bloody pitched battles, are vulnerable when facing the massed armies that the great powers can deploy.

WEAPONS

What would a man be without his blade? A simple working man will carry a knife, as much a tool as a weapon. A soldier might carry a larger fighting knife or a light main gauche to be held in the left hand, balancing a sword in the right or a sword-catcher with a broad hilt to entangle a foe's blade. An assassin would favour a slender *stiletto*, which slides as easily between the links of mail armour as it does between the ribs.

However, a gentleman bears a fine sword – a slender duelling rapier – which might be combined with a dagger, a second sword or even his cloak rolled round his left arm as an impromptu shield. For battle he carries a heavier arming sword more suited to fighting armoured foes, and may likewise wear a finely crafted suit of plate, if he can afford it. Single-shot wheel-lock pistols have a certain fashion, too, even though they are hardly honourable weapons.

For ordinary soldiers in the field, however, the typical melee weapons of the day are the sword (carried with a buckler, a small round or rectangular shield), the pike, the axe-bladed halberd, or the two-handed sword. The steel crossbow is still widely used, although the crude matchlock musket is now the main long-range weapon. Some peasant levies and mercenaries from the east still use bows. The most fortunate wear plate armour, but, for most, armour consists simply of a plate or chain hauberk and a helmet, and the least fortunate make do with a padded vest.

THE FLORENTINE ARSENAL

Of course, the red-and-white liveried professional soldiers of Florence and their allies have many unfair advantages. Most use the same weapons as their enemies, although perhaps their swords are turned out in the machine-shop assembly lines of Pistoia rather than being individually crafted. Increasingly, though, new weapons are making their way into common soldiers' hands, from spring-loaded multiple-shot crossbows to the prized new super-gun, the flintlock musket. Even more unusual weapons include hand-catapults firing grenades or glass globes of lethal or soporific vapours (neither especially popular nor successful, given their fragility), multi-barrelled light organ guns, silent spring grenades that hurl vicious shards in every direction when they trigger, and the exquisitely engraved *braccia lunga* (long arm), a combination flintlock and halberd borne by the republic's elite Signoria's Guard.

Likewise, alongside the simple cannon that most armies now deploy, Florence also utilises advanced guns with rifled barrels, as well as steam-powered crossbows, hand-cranked rotary organ guns, rockets with explosive warheads, wheel-mines that roll along the ground until their internal spring is discharged and then explode in gouts of flame or gas, and the fearsome steam-powered turtle-tanks.

The result has been that Florence's forces have enjoyed unprecedented success. When they pushed back the armies of Milan outside Pisa (and incidentally brought that rebellious city back under their thumb), they defeated a force three times their size in a single afternoon. However, they were fighting in ideal conditions – on the open plain, where their war machines could roam freely and the longer range of their weapons could make itself known, in sunny weather without rain to dampen the matchlocks of their muskets or fog to prevent the glider spotters from calling out targets to their rocket batteries. It would be foolish for Florence to assume that such circumstances will always prevail, but Machiavelli's warnings are increasingly falling on deaf ears as the other members of the Signoria become over-confident and downright acquisitive, thinking all Italy is at their feet.

STORY SEED: KING LOUIS SUPER-GUN

One of the great strengths of the French army is its cannon, which especially showed their value at the Battle of Fornovo in 1495. However, this is still essentially a battlefield asset, and a slow and temperamental one at that – cannon still have a depressing tendency to explode under pressure. Word comes to Florence that a new super-gun is under construction at a secret workshop somewhere along the shores of Lake Como, north of Milan: a weapon with a barrel 200 paces long and a bore that could swallow a cow. Is such a weapon possible? Could it throw a shell for leagues, or halfway across Italy? And how are they building it? It looks uncannily like the designs drawn up by Faustino d'Asti, set aside as impractical when he blew himself up along with several streets of Firenze Fuorimuri. Could the French have acquired the plans and worked out how to make them work? Indeed, could d'Asti have faked his own death and been working for the French ever since? Or is this just some wild plan that is making a fast-talking opportunist rich on King Louis' gold but has zero chance of real success? Someone has to find out, and, if need be, do something about this weapon.

MANO-A-MANO

Those fighting their foes hand-to-hand may rely on native strength, wit, and speed, but those looking for an edge may learn from the growing number of specialised schools of martial arts. There are fencing schools with their own tricks and techniques for both fighting dirty and courtly duelling. Whilst the earliest fencing manual dates back to the late thirteenth century, the invention of the printing press has better standardised these schools' techniques and led to their more widespread adoption. There are many different schools of fencing, each with their own distinctive moves and styles, but the most famous is the Dardi School, named after Lippo Dardi, a flamboyant and skilled swordsman who was also an astronomer and mathematics professor at the University of Bologna. This school trains its members in the use of the arming sword twinned with shield, knife, or impromptu defence.

There are also techniques such as the Sicilian peasant's *paranza* style of stick-fighting using a quarterstaff or a shorter baton, as well as knife-fighting techniques, although the latter are seen very much as the preserve of the *bravo* or the bandit. More widely practised are true unarmed combat styles, which are studied even by the nobility. After all, these are rough times and even a gentleman might just as easily find himself assailed by bandits as fighting a courtly duel. In such circumstances, boot, fist, and knife are most likely to be the weapons of availability, if not choice.

For all its folksy name, *calfi e schiaffi* (kicks and slaps) teaches a lethal, fluid mix of kicks and punches, whilst classical wrestling relies more on grappling with the opponent. However, as with so many other aspects of life, the New Science is bringing its own changes. Da Vinci himself had some contact with these martial disciplines (he was taught darts by the early Spanish fencing master, mathematician, and author Pietro Monte). Some comments of his one evening sparked inspiration for two of his students, each of whom is now developing their own 'martial science'. The soldier-turned-scholar Achille Marozzo has founded a school to teach *mano e mente* (hand and mind), an aggressive style that concentrates on exploiting pressure points and the limitations of the body to break bones, dislocate joints, and knock an enemy into unconsciousness or a paroxysm of pain with a surgically delivered punch. Alternatively, the flamboyant Agostini Fonte teaches *danza marziale* (martial dance), which relies on an understanding of geometry, momentum, and dynamics to redirect an attacker's own movement, sending them flying or immobilising them. Reflecting Fonte's own style, the movements of the danza are indeed based on the vigorous kicks and jumps of the popular dance known as the galliard.

TRAVEL

The lot of the commoner is still to walk on foot, or at best to ride on an oxcart; and to travel even the 42 miles between Florence and Pisa takes some 14 hours when walking at an average pace of 3 miles per hour. The rich and the mighty ride on horseback or travel by horse-drawn cart, but whilst these are much less tiring and far more comfortable, they are scarcely any faster, generally averaging 3–4 miles per hour at a walk. To be sure, a messenger willing to push their horse to the limit can get to Pisa in three or four hours – but the horse will then be exhausted.

TRAVEL DISTANCES BETWEEN MAIN CITIES (MILES)

	Bologna	Florence	Genoa	Mantua	Milan	Naples	Pisa	Rome	Siena	Torino	Venice
Bologna		68	187	71	134	361	111	237	107	206	97
Florence	68		145	127	190	296	52	171	43	261	161
Genoa	187	145		151	86	438	100	304	184	106	244
Mantua	71	127	151		117	420	170	296	176	173	97
Milan	134	190	86	117		483	173	358	228	95	167
Naples	361	296	438	420	483		346	144	268	555	455
Pisa	111	52	100	170	173	346		231	101	205	205
Rome	237	171	304	296	358	144	231		149	437	336
Siena	107	43	184	176	228	268	101	149		304	203
Torino	206	261	106	173	95	555	205	437	305		268
Venice	97	161	244	97	167	455	205	336	203	268	

However, the genius of the Rinascimento has brought unparalleled new options for travel on land, at sea, and even in the air! The new-fangled pedal-horse, for example, allows a person of strong calf-musculature to travel along smooth roads at the pace of a trotting horse, propelled simply by the rotary movement of the pedals. Alternatively, the even more advanced spring-horse allows one's natural strength to be assisted by the power of a tightly wound metal coil. Both types are sadly limited in their value by the dearth of smooth roads, however, with even cobbles prone to send an unskilled rider flying.

Steam-powered *vaporetti*, both smaller carriages suitable for conveying up to six gentlefolk of good means, or larger vehicles able to pull carts and barges, are now filling the air with steam and smoke from the coal- and wood-fired boilers that drive their engines. However prone they are to accidents, explosions, and discombobulations of their gears, they are less alarming than the latest (and rarest) *esplosivi* (explosives), whose infernal-combustion engines harness the power of detonating gunpowder to drive them at inhuman speeds, sometimes even as fast as 30 miles per hour, at least until they overturn or explode.

ON THE WATER

Barges and simple riverboats are a staple of inland goods transport and are growing in prevalence due to da Vinci's fascination with canals. Florence has begun building them to make the Arno River navigable to the sea, and with this change comes new vessels. An experimental venture has been the construction of three *fiumiculars* (as these new river-trains are known) by a private consortium backed by the Medici Bank. Workers in the hold or steam engines crank great gears that drive the wooden paddlewheels pushing these ungainly beasts through the water, even upstream, pulling barges laden with goods.

At sea, the relatively calm waters of the Mediterranean are still largely the domain of galleys propelled by banks of oars and large, triangular sails. War galleys mount simple cannon and carry soldiers for boarding actions – this is, after all, a time of piracy and raiding, especially between Christian and Muslim ships. The great galleys built by Venice and Genoa are some 180' long and propelled by 180 professional oarsmen. Most vessels are mercantile in nature, but those which are dedicated warships mount cannon firing 50-pound iron balls, as well as banks of smaller swivel guns. Ordinary galleys can still be up to 120' long, with 120–150 oarsmen, whilst smaller, faster and more manoeuvrable vessels – galliots, *fustas* and *bergantines*, in descending order of size – tend to be 50–90' long, with 30–80 oarsmen each. In every case, though, these ships are handsome works of art: brightly painted, gilded, and festooned with banners, silk hangings, and tapestries.

The great naval powers of the Mediterranean are Venice and the Ottoman Empire, followed by Genoa, Naples, Spain, the pirates of the Barbary Coast, and the Knights Hospitaller. Florence has never been a maritime state, but as its strength and ambitions grow, it is beginning to lay the keels for a new kind of vessel, the screwship – powered not by wind or oars, but by muscle, gears, and springs driving underwater propellers. These ships promise to make other vessels obsolete, not least by offering a flat platform for naval artillery, so Florence's rivals are duly concerned. On the other hand, they tend to scoff at the suggestion that the rising power is also working on a *sommersibile*, a vessel able to travel beneath the waves.

STORY SEED:
THE HUNT FOR RED OTTAVIO

STORY SEED:
THE HUNT FOR RED OTTAVIO

Florence's prototype *sommersibile* (submarine) is named *Red Ottavio* after Ottaviano de'Medici, an enthusiastic young scion of that line, who has thrown his lot in with the Republic. Or has he? The *Red Ottavio* is an exquisite confection of carved wood and burnished brass, its propeller and air pumps powered by pre-coiled springs and supplemented by a hand-crank. Crewed by a dozen stalwarts and captained by the doughty Capitano de'Marchi, the sommersibile set out secretly at drawn yesterday on its third shake-down cruise. On it was Ottaviano himself; having ploughed so much of his personal fortune and energy into the project, he could hardly be refused. The *Red Ottavio* ought to have returned at dusk. It is now the next day, and there is no sign of it. Is it now languishing on the bottom of the Mediterranean, having sprung a leak? Was it dragged off course by an unexpected current, now left becalmed at sea, its springs unwound? Florence's small navy is sending two fast galliots out to hunt for it, and the war galley *La Riga* is being signalled to quarter the waters off the Tuscan coast, but what if the *Red Ottavio* is headed to those pirates at Genoa? Or those murderous hypocrites in Rome? Maybe it is time some trusted people were sent up and down the coastline for any sight of this marvel, whilst others quietly make their way to Milan to listen for any rumours that Ottaviano was working for his kin there.

IN THE AIR

Perhaps the most extraordinary feats of the New Science are in transcending the bounds of the earth. Da Vinci's fascination with flight has led to the evolution of simple gliders, typically able to carry just one person. These *alianti* have become essential tools of the Signoria, carrying messages, watching the borders, and, in times of war, spying on the foe from the heavens. The glider pilots, typically daring young men of slender build and meagre weight so as not to overstress these fragile craft, are something of the social darlings of today's Florentine high society.

Meanwhile, a combination of the growing import of silks from distant China and new work on the dynamics of gases has been used by French-born Florentine artisan Marcel du Gras to make the first hot-air balloons. So far they are largely used for display or signalling, including lofting alarm lanterns at night, but du Gras dreams of the day when people may drift on the wind in one of his balloons.

Venice's nightmare is that Florence's new technologies will break their grip on the Mediterranean, and with good reason. Here, the sommersibile *Red Ottavio* closes in on a Venetian galley that, in turn, thought to take on a fully laden argosy merchantmen out of Dubrovnik, bringing salt, coal, and copper to Pisa. Shortly, the *Red Ottavio* will submerge, all the better to rip out the galley's keel from below.

MEDICINE

Renaissance medicine is not for the faint-hearted. Most doctors rely on a mix of herbal cures, folk remedies, and trial and error. Concepts of hygiene are primitive at best. Only a few avant-garde thinkers, such as Girolamo Fracastoro of Padua University, are talking about such concepts as germs, and Fracastoro is facing an uphill struggle to persuade people that what he calls the 'spores' bearing disease can be communicated not just directly – people do fear infection from the diseased – but through clothes and places.

Meanwhile, most medical thinking is based on the notion of 'humours', first developed in ancient Greece. The idea is that health depends on the right balance of the four fundamental fluids: blood, choler (yellow bile), black bile, and phlegm. Everyone naturally favours one more than the rest, which manifests itself in their complexion and character; thus, a preponderance of blood creates a 'sanguine' person, ruddy of looks and cheery of manner, whilst 'phlegmatics' tend to be pale and chilly, cholerics are short of temper, and those with too much black bile tend towards the dark and melancholy. Sickness results from 'dyscrasia': the body's fluids being out of the right balance because of diet or environmental factors, from being soaked in the rain to inhaling visible or invisible 'vapours' and 'miasmas'.

Treatment thus means attempts to get the humours back into balance. Some of this is pure quackery (like bleeding someone through small cuts to reduce their blood), but over the generations, through trial and error, some more useful remedies have emerged, such as using certain herbs and mixtures to treat fevers and infections. Nonetheless, a great deal of medicine is pretty hit or miss.

Likewise, surgery is often simple, amateurish, and dangerous. Amputations are largely carried out without any anaesthesia beyond strong drink, and the quicker the surgeon can complete the cutting and cauterise the wound with hot iron or boiling oil, the better the chance of survival. A great surgeon is a strong-armed butcher, able to saw through flesh and bone in less than half a minute. On the other hand, anatomy is a great fascination of the age. Despite the Church's disapproval, doctors and scholars flock to see dead bodies carefully dissected, hoping to learn the secrets of the human mechanism. To this end, there is even a thriving black market in corpses – with no questions asked, of course.

The opium poppy is the main sedative of the time, and a highly prized commodity. It is not yet smoked in Europe the way it is sometimes done in the East (although there are addicts, largely wealthy, who take it several times a day, drunk in a tincture), but someone has stumbled on the refined form of opium known as morphine. That someone may be the young prodigy Paracelsus, who has just moved to the University of Ferrara to study for his doctorate. Or perhaps it is the scholarly nun Salvaza at the nunnery of the Church of Santa Maria Novella in Florence, which sustains itself by its pharmaceutical workshop, producing and selling cosmetics, distilled water, and other compounds. Being outside the control of the guilds and having to compete with their more established monkish rivals, the nuns are perhaps more willing to experiment in the giddy environment of novelty and invention now ruling Florence.

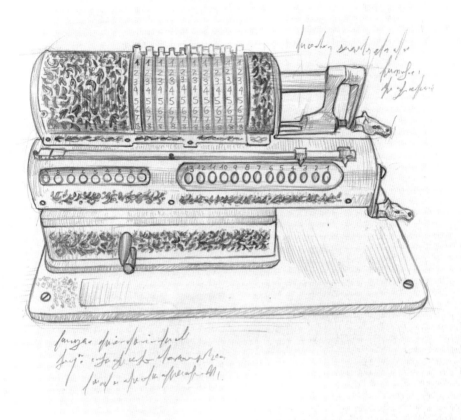

Instead of their abacuses, the most forward-thinking of bankers tally their profits and losses on a pinwheel calculator like this one, made for the chief cashier of the Gondi Bank. Mechanical Abacus +3d.

SCHOLARSHIP

The great universities of the time are simultaneously havens of conservative orthodoxy, radical free thinking, and mindless hedonism (so unlike the modern world). Students typically enrol at age 14 or 15 and take four years to get their bachelor's degree, studying the seven liberal arts: arithmetic, astronomy, geometry, music theory, grammar, rhetoric, and, above all, formal logic, all heavily taught through the works of the classical writers of the ancient world. Upon graduating, most will then leave, but some will stay on and spend up to another twelve years pursuing a master's degree or doctorate in one of three subjects: law, medicine, or theology.

Students generally come from well-to-do stock, as they must pay their tutors as well as keep body and soul together, but they do have the advantage of getting the same legal protection as the clergy during their studies. In other words, they cannot be tried in secular courts, only in church ones, and thus cannot face corporal punishment. What this does tend to mean is that for every hard-working soul who gets up by candlelight for classes that start at dawn, there is some spoiled, high-born wastrel who parties and wenches all night and doesn't even pretend to study by day. So long as the dues are paid, they can stay at university for years. They'll presumably rely on their family to find something to do, but for their more scholarly peers a career in the Church, law, business, or medicine beckons.

The oldest university in the world is in Bologna. It is more than 400 years old and even more venerable than Paris and Oxford. Italy's other notable universities are at Padua (renowned equally for its research in anatomy and science and the unruly nature of its students and faculty – it is currently virtually on strike because of efforts by the Church to rein in its intellectual adventurousness), Siena (which unusually provides bursaries for poor but able students, thanks to a tax levied by the city authorities), Florence (which is a cradle of the New Science) and Rome (where La Sapienza University is under the patronage of the Pope, with all the perks and restrictions that entails).

PARACELSUS, PRECOCIOUS POLYMATH

Physician, occultist, alchemist, toxicologist, and botanist 'Paracelsus' – his real name is the splendidly polysyllabic Philippus Aureolus Theophrastus Bombastus von Hohenheim – is an insufferably precocious German-Swiss polymath who has just moved to the University of Ferrara to study for his doctorate, at age 17. His brilliance is surpassed only by his ego, but if you can cope with his sharp tongue and open disdain for anyone who disagrees with him, it is amazing what he can do and teach, especially for a teenager.

Body 1, Mind 6, Soul 2. Brilliant Scientist 7d, Ground-breaking Doctor 5d, Astronomer 5d, Astrologer 5d, Spotty Teenager 4d, Arrogant Pain in the Backside 8d

LAW AND CRIME

In most cities, maintaining order and upholding the law is in the hands of magistrates elected from the well-to-do citizenry. Some are hard-working, intelligent, and know the law; others exploit their positions ruthlessly to take bribes and prosecute personal vendettas; then there are some who consider it a tedious social duty and spend as little time on it as possible. The exception is Venice, where the State Inquisition is at once both a professional magistracy and a political police. Either way, magistrates rely on not only the law and their wits but also informants and the use of torture to compel confessions, including the infamous *strappado*: tying a suspect's wrists behind their back and then hoisting the suspect off the ground, time and again, until they confess.

These magistrates are assisted by forces of patrollers and constables recruited from the poor, who likewise range from drunkards and the dregs of society to occasional dedicated professionals. Again, the Venetians have the largest and best trained forces. The constables of Milan and Florence are fairly well regarded, but only by the standards of the time – they are still often inexperienced, corrupt, unprofessional, and overstretched. All the same, they are better than the *sbirri*, the Roman constables, who are so notoriously corrupt, high-handed, and unpopular that the worst insult prostitutes can throw at each other is 'sbirro's girlfriend'.

The authorities do what they can to preserve law and order, but in practice most criminals are dealt with either informally (a good kicking, maybe, or having to pay their victims over and above what they stole) or through fines, public humiliation (pictures of convicted wrong-doers are painted in public places, such as on the walls of Florence's Bargello, with details of the crimes), or even a whipping. More serious punishments are largely reserved for professional criminals or those from out of town, and these can be savage. In Florence, debtors and petty criminals are more likely to end up working off their dues or fines in state farms or Le Gigli. Those convicted of murder, banditry, or the like face torture, maiming, and a painful death, often as a public spectacle before a jeering mob.

The main crimes are thefts, robberies, and outbreaks of impromptu violence caused by real or imagined sleights – this is, after all, a time of thin skins and touchy honour. States try to reduce the risks through measures such as controlling weapons. In Rome, concealable weapons like wheel-lock carbines are banned, and some others are licensed but even then cannot legally be carried at night. In Bologna, carrying a ladder during the hours of darkness is a serious offence, as it suggests an intent to burgle. Siena goes even further, with a dusk-to-dawn curfew for everyone except night-watchmen, doctors, and refuse collectors.

Cities are generally small, but large enough that it is possible to hide in them after committing a crime – although if the authorities really want to find you then eventually they will. After all, too many people know too many others, strangers are often objects of curiosity, and there are only so many places you can buy food or seek shelter. So if you really want to be safe, you get out. Given that Italy is a patchwork of independent city states, fleeing for only a few miles or hours can often get you into the jurisdiction of a neighbouring city. This can well mean safety, especially if the two cities are not allies.

Of course, the authorities know this too, and often take steps to prevent precisely this. The most advanced response is in Florence. There, when a serious crime is discovered, three cannon shots are fired as an alarm. At once, the city gates are closed to anyone without a special permit to leave, river traffic along the Arno is halted, and barges are inspected before they can pass on. Officials of neighbouring villages will ring the church bells to rally local farmers to assemble to help search for fugitives. Although it is not impossible to lie low inside the city, this is a remarkably organised system for its time, especially now that the Catalogo means that everyone must carry an identity card. Furthermore, especially dangerous criminals may be watched for from the air by gliders and find themselves pursued by clockwork carriages, clicking and clattering along the roads behind them. Of course, criminals who are well prepared could seek to use such methods themselves.

Crime is hardly confined to the cities, though. This is also a time when banditry is rife across the countryside. Sometimes, cities will send patrols out to try and find and engage bandit gangs when they become especially dangerous, but more often it is simply the case that travellers have to accept the risks and make sure they have their knife or a stout stick to hand. Of course, those with most to lose, such as aristocrats and tax collectors, will make sure they travel with well-armed guards.

LORENZO NERONI, RUTHLESS VENETIAN MAGISTRATE

Half secret policeman, half thief-catcher, Neroni understands the truth well, and it takes such an understanding to know how to make it dance and sing when the interests of the Venetian state demand it. As an adolescent, he watched his aristocratic family be all but destroyed and his father forced to slash his wrists in appeasement when lie after lie turned a petty infraction into a treasonous scandal. Since then, he has always rigidly told the truth, even if his brooding and mercurial intellect is well versed in how to shade and trim the truth to mislead. He is one of the most relentless and feared magistrates of the Venetian Inquisition. Whilst he will do whatever is necessary to protect the state, Neroni is an honourable man, as willing to tackle corruption in the Grand Council as a backstreet murder. A man like that must be driven by restless inner demons and make many enemies, not that any such turmoil or uncertainty makes it past his perfectly controlled exterior.

Body 4, Mind 6, Soul 4. Man of the Truth 7d, Perceptive Investigator 7d, Ruthless 5d, Many an Enemy 6d, Self-control 5d, I Am an Agent of the Venetian State 7d, Inner Demons 6d

Foul Paolo is a fixture in the alleys of Rome, from whom gentlefolk avert their eyes with disgust (which is just as well, as his array of apparent sores and growths seems to change from day to day). Is he just a beggar on the make, or a spy, or maybe a lookout for one of the Eternal City's dangerously powerful crime gangs?

VICE

Prostitution is considered a sin, but an unavoidable one. Humans are just too flawed – and anyway, as almost every city government argues, why not tax the wages of sin? Most towns and cities have public, licensed brothels tucked discreetly away from the main piazzas and thoroughfares, although there are also unlicensed prostitutes and brothels aplenty. Rome's Campo Marzo is infamous as the red light district of choice for the Vatican, but Venice has the reputation for the most numerous and the least inhibited prostitutes, both male and female. It has legalised and registered them – there are officially over 11,000 prostitutes in Venice, a city of 100,000 – but, in fairness, many of these are opportunistic part-timers or cater to the city's many visitors. Courtesans are rather different, ranging from upmarket escorts hired as elegant and witty adornments to their patrons, through to the semi-permanent mistresses of the mighty. Often, they are figures of wealth and influence and, again, dissolute Venice is (in)famous for the number, power, and seductive expertise of its courtesans.

Gambling is equally rife, and most city governments seem to be more bothered by this than by prostitution – probably because it distracts the lower orders and drives aristocrats into debt. However, it thrives in every quarter, from the elite card- and dice-gaming houses known as *ridotti* to impromptu street-corner games. Professional gamblers, cheats, and loan sharks prey on this passion, and ordinary Italians seem to be willing to wager on anything. For example, in the often-bloody game of *civettino*, two men stand toe to toe and try to be the first to knock the other's hat off with slaps and punches, whilst a crowd gather to bet and heckle.

IMPERIA, FAMED ROMAN COURTESAN

A legendary beauty who invented black silk sheets to better contrast with her pale skin, 'Imperia'– Lucrezia de Parigi of Ferrara – is a renowned figure in Roman high society: her clients are bankers, cardinals, and princes. Despite her lavish lifestyle, she is exceedingly rich – not just in money and possessions, but also in gossip and secrets extracted from her clients. At 35, she is arguably at her peak, but she is clearly concerned – obsessed, even – by what her fate will be once her physical charms begin to fade and someone younger, prettier, and newer takes her place. She has some scheme, or many schemes, in mind. There is talk of money hoarded and then transferred in mysterious transactions, of midnight meetings on abandoned bridges, of messages to and from the capitals of the world and obscure mountain villages alike. Does Imperia have political ambitions? Is she taking over a bank? Will she find some eminent husband (some claim that England's Henry VIII has made overtures, although he is already married, so this must be a mistake)? Is she bankrolling alchemists working on the elixir of life? She would make an unusual patron, ally, or contact, and a subtle enemy.

Body 2, Mind 5, Soul 4. Legendary Beauty 10d, Font of Insider Gossip 7d, Wraps Men around Her Little Finger 7d, Worried about the Future 6d, Wealth 6d

THE CHURCH AND FAITH

With the exception of relatively small communities professing other faiths, this is a time when pretty much everyone in Europe follows the teachings of the Catholic Church. To be blunt, it is dangerous not to. However, quite what that means varies wildly: there are fervent believers, there are those who pay lip-service to the faith whilst not really believing in it, and most are somewhere in between. They believe in God, they pray, they pay their tithes to the Church, but it is not a primary force in their lives.

There have been church reform movements in the past, such as the Hussites of fifteenth-century Bohemia, but these have been crushed with ruthless zeal. However, the Renaissance is an era in which old truths are being reassessed and questioned. A very few free thinkers are wondering whether there is a God at all, but more common is discontent with the direction of the Catholic Church and what are seen as its betrayals and distortions of true Christian values. Savonarola was one such free thinker, and in the German city of Wittenburg, a rising theologian by the name of Martin Luther is engaged in the soul-searching that will soon lead to the major schism within European Christianity known as the Reformation.

But for now, Christianity in Europe essentially means Catholicism – and that means the Papacy. The Papacy is so much more than just a religious institution; it is an empire, with a series of Papal States and dependencies kept in check by an army of levies and mercenaries. It is a commercial superpower, rich from taxes, from tithes drawn from across Christendom, and from the sale of indulgencies promising that the punishment sinners face in the afterlife can be reduced by the payment of suitable fees.

The Papacy is also, frankly, deeply corrupt. Not every Pope or cardinal, perhaps, but even rising into the senior ranks of the church depends more on politics, patronage, and out-and-out bribery than faith. Papal armies go to war in the name of dynastic interests, Popes elevate their family members to be cardinals, and the lords of the Church live lives as pampered and privileged as any aristocrat. The current Pope, Julius II, is less interested in personal gain than in power and prestige, and is proving a key player in Italian politics. Even so, for all the status and wealth of the Papacy, the more far-sighted of its officials do worry that a storm is on the horizon.

Of course, the world of the Vatican and the lives of the princes of the Church are far removed from the lives of most who work for the faith. The local priest is not just a religious figure but a community leader, a mediator between the authorities and his flock, and a source of comfort in tough times. Only men can become priests, and they commit themselves (though not always successfully) to a life of celibacy and devotion. So too do the monks and nuns of various orders, such as those of St Augustus and St Francis. They do not simply contemplate the infinite, however; they provide care for the sick, support for the poor, and a refuge for the desperate. They need to raise funds for their institutions, which means they grow crops, brew beer, press wine, sell honey, and offer their services as letter-writers and accountants. They are also often devoted to literacy, learning, or even science.

THE 'OTHER'

HERETICS

The Pope may fancy himself spiritual lord over a unified faith, but the discontent that will soon lead to the Reformation and the ensuing bloody Wars of Religion is already evident. There is much unhappiness with the greed and corruption of the Church, with the way clerical offices are bought and sold, and with how pardons for sins are weaponised for political gain. Beyond that, though, there are all kinds of sects and movements that the Church considers heretical: some genuinely radical, others simply defined by some seemingly trivial detail of doctrine. The Fraticelli (Little Brothers) preach that the wealth of the Church is a sin, for example, but the Obversi simply obsess that the sign of the cross should only be performed with the left hand.

These movements tend to appeal most to artisans and the more skilled craftspeople, and for them the Church reserves its most bitter rage. There is no centralised 'Roman Inquisition' in Italy – this is not like Spain – nor is there the fad for witch-hunting (and burning). However, local religious authorities will convene their own Inquisitions and tribunals, especially calling on the doctrinal rigidity of the Dominican and Franciscan Orders, and the specialist skills of torturers, to force suspects into confession, often followed by a painful death. No wonder most sects operate deeply undercover.

JEWS

This is a time when Jews across Europe, including Italy, face prejudice and discrimination. Adult Jews are meant to wear a yellow 'o' the size of the palm of a hand on their clothes and are sometimes restricted from certain professions, but in the main they are free to live where they choose (there are no ghettos, although until recently Venice did not allow Jews to live on its main island), and they can work how and where they will. Indeed, when Spain expelled its Jewish population in 1492, Pope Alexander VI declared that they were 'permitted to lead their lives free from interference from Christians, to continue in their own rites, [and] to enrich themselves'. Some fear that this may change, as the Spanish influence grows and the Church becomes more intolerant, but, conversely, the new spirit of the times flowing from Florence is one of acceptance. Known for being scholars, physicians, and accountants, many Jews are finding new opportunities for themselves in the New Science and the economic boom it is generating.

MUSLIMS

There may be very few Muslims in Italy at this time, but their influence is everywhere – the peninsula's position at the heart of the Mediterranean, as well as the temporary Arab dominance over Sicily, has exposed Italy to influences from the east for centuries. For most Italians, Muslims are a distant menace: whilst a thousand Muslims is an invading army, the odd one or two are little more than strange foreigners with their own strange ways, arguably no more foreign than a Scotsman or a Pole. There are not even particular laws defining their status, because apart from some mercenaries and traders from the Ottoman-held parts of the Balkans, there are too few to merit it. That said, these are suspicious and superstitious times. If anything untoward should happen, passing Muslims are more likely to be blamed on principle, and the more hard-line clergy might not hesitate to encourage their flocks to drive out the 'Saracen'.

HANDLING TRICKY TOPICS

This information is presented to give you a sense of the customs and values of the times, however problematic they are today. Inevitably, the setting of *Gran Meccanismo*, rooted as it is in history, touches on some topics and attitudes that we find deeply problematic today, from the treatment of the Jews to gender relations. Remember: this is your game, your world, your gaming group. What each group does with it is up to them. Some may want to lean into this issue, or indeed make it an important motivating theme, such as the struggles of Jews to progress and even push back against prejudiced treatment. Others may find it a distraction at best, disturbing at worst. In this situation, you can dial down or even exclude those topics that are problematic. That's fine, too. What is crucial is that everyone is comfortable with whatever decision is made, and this is often best handled by an open discussion before the game begins, to ascertain everyone's comfort levels.

When Trivulzio sent his forces to try and 'save' Pisa from Florentine oppression (read: replace it with Milanese oppression), he gave Machiavelli a perfect opportunity to showcase the Republic's new might. Here, the turtle-tank *Aquila Florentiae* is breaking a pike-and-musket line to allow the Second Santa Croce Militia to roll up the Milanese flank, triggering a general rout.

THE GAME

"I think it may be true that Fortune is the arbiter of half of our actions, but that she still leaves the other half of them, more or less, to be governed by us."

- Niccolò Machiavelli, The Prince

This book gives you all the tools you need to tell exciting collaborative stories with a group of friends. This is a roleplaying game where one player, named the Guide, is responsible for designing the setting, the antagonists, the situations, and the adventures that the other players will discover and resolve. The other players, usually from 2 to 5, will each play as a single character during the game, acting and speaking as them as they interact with the world and the other characters: both those played by the other players and the Guide.

Gran Meccanismo uses Graham Spearing's TRIPOD game engine. TRIPOD is a mnemonic for Traits In Pools Of Dice, a system designed for fun, descriptive, and creative narrative-driven play. This game uses descriptive phrases – 'Traits' – and applies them directly to play by giving each phrase a value, which is converted into a number of six-sided dice that you throw when resolving Challenges. The game rules are a refinement of an earlier edition called *Wordplay*.

A ROLEPLAYING GAME SESSION

A typical game session will take between two and four hours to complete, typically an evening's or afternoon's play. Several sessions will often be spent playing through a particular story – although there may be no distinct structure of defined 'stories' or 'scenarios', but rather a constant flow of evolving narrative. For example, the players might have been engaged to escort a noblewoman to Milan, where she is to be married. Depending on what happens along the way and the complexity of the story, this could be resolved in a single session, or it could alternatively take many if she is abducted by a rival suitor, the characters have to track them down and free her, and they then need to resolve the ensuing potential political crisis when the noblewoman reveals that she had always intended to elope with the rival anyway.

The Guide has a central role, providing and describing the setting for the game. These elements are usually planned and developed before the actual game session commences. The Guide will also draft a backstory and plot with hooks for the players to explore using their characters, created using the guidance in this book.

During the game, players will move in and out of character. When describing actions, asking questions about rules, or going off on a tangent, the player will speak with their own voice. When 'being' their character during play and speaking to other characters, the player will speak in the first person as if they were the character. Some players find that using colourful accents and amateur dramatics helps to 'show off' their game character – however, these techniques are entirely optional!

Players are not passive consumers of the setting and story conceived by their Guide; they also create their own stories and objectives to pursue, which they play out to further develop their character and the shared game world. A great deal of the fun of the game is to be found when players create and sustain believable and enjoyable characters who will live long in the memory even after the game itself has finished. Players will also suggest scenery and atmosphere to use as part of their actions, enriching the setting.

The 'game' element consists of a set of rules that use the details on the players' character sheets to determine the numbers of dice that the players will roll to find out if their character successfully achieves what they have described in play. A range of factors affect these dice rolls, including the difficulty of the endeavour and the capabilities of the character.

The Republic of Florence

in its might and majesty, under God and through the
will of its people, grants the rights and duties of
citizenship and residence, unalienably, hereunto:

Eleonora Mori

For the Republic
Nicholo mckiavelly B:
Commissioner for Peace and War

Tessera | 0 | 3 | 4 | 0 | 0 | 1 | 7 | 2 |

Il Catalogo Statale

Il Catalogo Statale

It is a mark of pride for every Florentine citizen to carry their
Catalogo identity card. By order of the State.

THE BASICS

To help resolve Challenges and understand how individuals, forces, and influences affect each other, the game assigns numerical values to short descriptive phrases known as Traits.

The rules are based around using these phrases - Traits - directly in play. Everything that you can describe in your game can have Traits: locations, characters, personal items, mood, and atmosphere. Most people and things can be described in essence by one or a few such Traits.

Player characters and some others – the people and constructs that really matter in the story (think of the named characters in a film or TV programme, rather than the extras described as 'second soldier' or 'woman in hat') – will also have Attributes. An Attribute provides a core capability when resolving a Challenge, the name given to the various kinds of tests and conflicts that characters will face. Player characters have three Attributes – Body, Mind, and Soul – broadly reflecting their physical, mental, and moral strength, but other aspects of the world may have their own attributes that allow them to be challenged, used, or otherwise involved in play.

Traits and Attributes are given a numeric strength, which indicates how potent they will be in play. We will discuss how they are used later in the book.

Example: The action in the game is taking place within a wild storm. This could simply be used as a Trait for the scene: Wild Storm 3d. In play, the Wild Storm could be used by a player or the Guide either to provide a bonus of three dice to a character's dice pool or to increase the Difficulty of an action by the same amount, adding the dice to the opposing Difficulty pool.

If, for some reason, it is dramatically appropriate to make it more of a central challenge, the storm could also be thought of as a character with an Attribute and a series of associated Traits: Attribute: Wild Storm 3d; Traits: Howling Wind 2d, Crackling Lightning 3d, Endless Swirling Rain 4d.

The Wild Storm can now be used like a character in play, using its core Attribute along with one or another of its Traits to unnerve and impede the player characters, or possibly to be used by them to their advantage. We'll see more about this when we look at Challenges.

Scale (p. 144) is also used to provide a game effect for things that can use their sheer size or power as an advantage in Challenges.

Guide characters are called Non-Player Characters, or NPCs for short. NPCs, especially those who won't appear for very long in the game, are generally prepared using a simple shorthand with just a single Trait. So, for example, a penny-pinching clerk could simply be Penny-Pinching Clerk 5d. If our penny-pinching clerk asked to do something that doesn't fit very well with that description, then simply reduce the Trait by one or more dice, depending on how far from the clerk's usual activities it may be. NPCs who are especially significant can be prepared quickly in a more detailed format, with three Attribute scores and some Traits with values to go with them.

When a character finds themselves in an uncertain situation that contains risk, known as a Challenge, the player whose character is being tested and the Guide each roll a handful of six-sided dice. The number of dice the player uses is calculated by adding up one Attribute, one appropriate character Trait, and possibly one other Trait taken from the surrounding scene or some useful equipment or tools, and any supporting friends' actions. The Guide's dice come either from one of their characters in the same way, or from a set Difficulty for the Challenge.

After rolling, any dice showing a 4 or 5 count as one success each, and any dice showing a six count as two successes. The side with the greater number of successes wins. If there is a tie then the Guide will adjudicate the outcome based on what they think is most interesting for the story, often allowing the hero to succeed – but with some new complication.

> **Example:** *Vittorio the down-on-his luck painter is trying to persuade the aloof Countess of Orvieto to become a patron. Vittorio is trying to inspire her with his artistic vision, so he is using his Soul Attribute of 3 and his Always Enthusiastic 3d Trait. The Guide decides he gets one extra die from his surroundings, as he has managed to meet the Countess in her rather dilapidated audience chamber, which could do with a make-over. The Countess of Orvieto is resisting with her Aloof 4d.*
>
> *The player throws seven dice and gets the following results: 6,4,3,3,2,1,1 – the 6 gives two successes, the 4 gives one success, and the other five dice don't give any, so the final result is three successes. The Guide rolls four dice: 5,4,4,1 – which is also a total of three successes. The Guide decides that the countess is sceptical, but nevertheless allows Vittorio to start work on the chamber – on the condition that she will pay only if she likes the outcome. Vittorio has a job, but still nowhere to eat or sleep!*

We will cover the rules for Challenges in more detail later (p. 121). Next, we will show you how to create memorable player characters, whose exploits you will describe as they live their eventful lives in the Guide's setting.

The Milanese bitterly call it the 'dawn chorus' – the early morning hubbub as Swiss mercenaries kick down another suspected revolutionary's door to take them away for questioning or worse. Here, they are accompanied by a street-corner radical who 'volunteered' to turn informant after only a couple of nights spent in the cells of the Sforza Castle.

THE CHARACTERS

"The lion cannot protect himself from traps, and the fox cannot defend himself from wolves. One must therefore be a fox to recognize traps, and a lion to frighten wolves."

- Niccolo Machiavelli, *The Prince*

The players in a game of *Gran Meccanismo* control the main characters. These characters are the focus of the story that the gaming group will tell together, whether they be heroes or anti-heroes. All the information about your character is recorded on a character sheet, an example of which is shown on page 190 (and is also available online at ospreypublishing.com/gaming_resources_roleplaying). This chapter takes you through the process of creating a player character.

TRAITS

As well as their three basic Attributes – Body, Mind, and Soul – player characters, like everything and everyone else in the game, are defined by Traits. Any descriptive phrase or ability can be a Trait. Traits should be noticeable attributes that are likely to have an impact during a game session. These words and numbers are recorded on the character sheet, which serves to lay out all the crucial factors that contribute to describing the character in one place. Some Traits describe how the character looks or acts, whilst others summarise their personal history or skills. Some will be positive, whilst others will be negative.

Traits are given a numeric value between 1 and 12 (generally not starting above 5), representing how much the Trait will help a character to succeed at Challenges. A Trait with a value of 1 is very weak and probably will not be used to any great success (other than for comic value) in any testing situations. A Trait of 12 is as powerful as it can get. It is very rare to find anything with a Trait that high. As the number denotes the number of dice, a 'd' is placed after the number in this context. So, a character might have the following:

Mind Trait: Obsessed with Clockwork 4d

An average, unnamed Guide character will usually have a value of 3 for most of their Traits, or perhaps a 4 in one of them to denote expertise or a particularly noteworthy ability. Player characters and named Guide characters will tend to have more Traits and at higher levels.

Traits are grouped by Attribute:

Body Traits: How a character looks and moves. *For example: Agile, Arresting Gaze, Big-fisted, Cat-like Grace, Comfortably Girthed, Curvaceous Figure, Dancer, Darting Rapier, Drinks Like a Fish, Enormous Beard, Graceful, Run for My Life, Tall, Twinkle in the Eye, Well-preserved.*

Mind Traits: Knowledge, deductive abilities, intelligence, and perception. *For example: Airhead, Architect, Clever, Cunning as a Fox, Deduce the Truth, Expert in Canon Law, Find My Way, Herbalist, Knows [specialist subject], Latin Grammar, Navigation, Perfect Memory, Sharp Eyes, Smooth Liar, Vacuous.*

Soul Traits: Personality, passions, artistic and social abilities, and relationships. *For example: Artistic, Bold, Bombastic, Convincing, Don't Look at Me, Garrulous, Gentle, Love My Mum, Loved by the People of Spoleto, People Watching, See Every Angle, Shy Crush on Maria diPaoli, Streetwise, Watercolour Painter, Zealous Christian.*

You could be forgiven for wondering if some of these examples are a little too flowery. After all, why bother with *Darting Rapier* when you could just have *Swordfighting*? You are entirely free to stick to simpler language, but choosing more evocative terms doesn't just help flesh out your character – in this case, he is clearly an elegant and swift swordsman rather than just a brutally effective hacker and slasher – it can sometimes be useful. For example, if you found yourself needing to quickly catch a glass vial of poison before it smashes on the tiled floor, you could conceivably make a case that *Darting Rapier* demonstrates quick hands and would come into play; it is up to the Guide to decide if they will accept that and what kind of penalty there will be for using it in this out-of-context way. However, they are much less likely to buy any attempt to use *Swordfighting* in such a situation.

Traits may also sometimes seem to overlap between types. *Poker Face, Convincing Liar*, and *Trustworthy Manner* may all be used to fast-talk your way past the guard at the city gate, but as Body, Mind, and Soul Traits respectively, they offer nuanced takes on the same basic characteristic. For example, a poker face won't be that useful when you are trying to convince the poisoner's sister that you have fallen for her and you are asking her ever so sweetly to help you find the antidote.

Likewise, some Traits could fit into more than one category. For example, if *People Watching* is placed in Mind, you are emphasising perception: the ability to notice and decode particular behaviours and mannerisms. On the other hand, if it is placed in Soul, you are emphasising the interpretative nature of the Trait – intuitively recognising why someone is behaving in a certain way.

Traits are used continuously throughout a game. They highlight how your character can interact with the game world and influence the shared story, acting as the keys to bringing your character off the page and into the heart of the action around the table. They are entered on the character sheet for reference during the game. Get to know your character Traits and make them your own – you're going to be using them a lot.

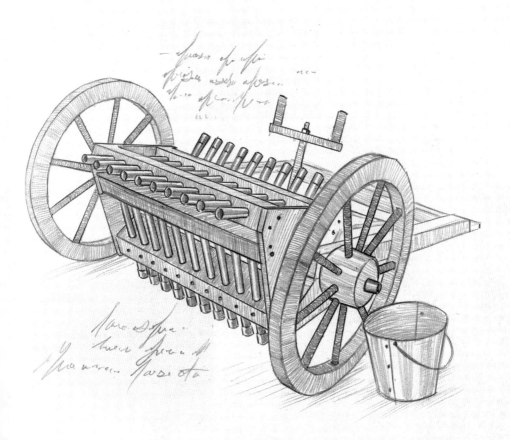

The terrible virtue of da Vinci's organ gun is that as the gun is cranked, and as each of the three banks of eleven barrels fire, the next bank is being loaded. It can lay down murderous volley after murderous volley, until the handmade cartridges run out or the weapon overheats – hence the bucket of water kept close to hand.

FLAWS

Flaws are Traits that describe a negative aspect of a character. From one point of view, they are Traits that are not useful to have; however, as in real life, Flaws can add a defining and interesting signature to a character, giving their personality a rounded feel and usually making play more fun. A Flaw can, from a different perspective, have a positive side that can be used to great effect in a game. Greed, hatred, jealousy, or obsession, whilst clouding a character's judgment, can be used to drive the game powerfully down certain avenues, and a Flaw like *Timorous 2d* might be useful if the character is being tempted into a trap.

There will come a time when a character's Flaw is extremely helpful to an opposing character or situation. When this happens, a player can voluntarily announce the Flaw to the Guide and offer it as a bonus to their opponent in a Challenge. The player character may gain a reward for doing so, as explained in the Advancement section (p. 158). Alternatively, the Guide may look through a character's Traits and pick out one that will help them win a Challenge against the player's character. The effect of this is explained in Building Your Pool of Dice (p. 126).

SUPPORTING CHARACTERS

Any Trait that identifies an individual permits the player to create a supporting character with a single, easy-to-apply Trait. For example, the swashbuckling Mantuan soldier of fortune and poet Francesco di Polli has his *Devoted Valet Mercurio* 4d as a Soul Trait. The long-suffering manservant could simply be treated as a regular NPC – *Mercurio* 4d – and thus roll four dice when facing relevant Challenges in the game.

However, the player or Guide may wish to have their supporting character be partially or fully fleshed out. If so, Mercurio could become a separate character, subsidiary to the main hero, with 2–4 Traits averaging 4d. Perhaps, for example, he could have *Annoyingly Cheerful at All Times* 3d, *I Know Someone Who Can Get Their Hands on That* 4d, *Patience of a Saint* 5d, and *Spit and Polish* 4d. If it was really wanted, Mercurio could be given Body, Mind, and Soul Attributes, though it is worth noting that in this case he would be much more capable when operating independently.

The player can usually dictate the actions of the hero's supporting characters, but getting them to do something especially unusual, dangerous, or distasteful will require a Challenge testing the strength of the relationship against a Difficulty based on just how far this action would go against the supporting character's interests or instincts. The Guide may reduce the level of the relationship, either permanently or temporarily, if the hero abuses it. For example, Mercurio is used to covering up his master's romantic indiscretions and this does not generally require a Challenge. However, when Francesco tries to get him to help cover up the cold-blooded murder of the husband of one of his conquests, that offends his sensibilities – the Guide requires Francesco to pit his 4d relationship against Mercurio's outrage, which they choose to set at 4d as well.

If Francesco fails by a narrow margin, Mercurio refuses, with the relationship suffering a 'wound' representing the damage done to the bond between them. A disastrous failure might finally open Mercurio's eyes to his master's true nature and have him running to the authorities or simply leaving, never to shine Francesco's boots again.

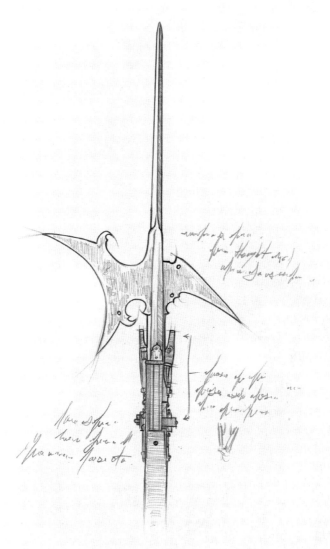

The red-tunicked Signoria's Guard carry the braccia lunga, the 'long arm', combining halberd and paired flintlocks. Gun-axe +3d

Manfredo Manfredi, the old soldier turned Florentine gunsmith, is known for his ingenious new weapons, such as this three-barrel repeater. Indeed, such is his skill that it is said he is the armourer for the secret agents of the Signoria.

CREATING YOUR CHARACTER

Where do you start when making a character for *Gran Meccanismo*? A good place is to start with a concept, typically a single sentence that gives a broad sense of the character. Then, determine the character's Attributes. Next, determine Traits, for which the standard way is to use one of the Archetypes and Origins that follow, then decide how to personalise them. You can start with a narrative in mind or simply with a general concept, as explained below. It can be useful for a group to create characters together so that they can write in associations and conflicts between the player characters right from the start – shared goals can be a powerful way of cementing the group. However, although it is problematic to have a group of player characters who hate each other or have nothing in common, there is also a place for disparate priorities or rivalries – just be sure that, ultimately, the characters have more reasons to work together than to squabble or separate.

In some games, especially one-off games run at conventions, the players may be given pre-generated characters, but in the main it is best if the players have as much control over creating characters as they want. The more creative ownership and engagement they feel, the better. A selection of pre-generated characters for your use, as well as a blank character sheet, is available on the Osprey Games website, ospreypublishing. com/gaming_resources_roleplaying.

1. CONCEPT

This concept will get fleshed out as you choose an Archetype and Origins in the later steps, but it is best to start with a line or two that sums up the character in a nutshell, such as:

> *A Venetian naval captain and art collector, who hides his ruthless greed behind an extravagantly courteous manner.*

> *Too outspoken and independent for the convent, a former nun who now masquerades as a man, making a living as a fence in the margins of the Roman underworld.*

> *An absent-minded scholar, whose mathematical skill has led her to be employed as a cryptographer by the Florentine government.*

> *A battle-scarred Swiss mercenary who cannot go home until he has found a wife.*

For long-running games, it is entirely conceivable that a character's concept will change over the course of the stories that you create at the game table.

Some players want to go a little further, such as:

Bruno de Gasperi is a man with ambitions, a Florentine banker who sees in the new clockwork revolution a chance to make a fortune, to marry off his blind sister Isabella well, and to finally have his revenge on the Orsinis.

We get a sense of who Bruno is and what matters to him, but we don't know if he is unprincipled or honourable, or what he has against the Orsinis. That's fine – these details can be dealt with later. Indeed, the player themself may not have a clear and comprehensive idea, but it may emerge in time.

Players may even wish to write a few paragraphs of rich description and backstory, especially using words and phrases that can be taken as Traits:

No one seeing the sleekly elegant Bruno de Gasperi, rising star of the Florentine banking community, would believe the murderous hunger for revenge that burns inside him. As a young man, he loved a woman from afar, Angelina Petrocchi, the daughter of a minor city official. Angelina unexpectedly married Francesco Orsini, younger son of the powerful mercenary family, in what Bruno is convinced was an arranged match against her will. The 17-year-old Bruno tried to challenge him to a duel, only to be beaten and thrown aside by Francesco's guards, badly hurt, as Francesco was hurriedly hustled out of the city to avoid a diplomatic incident. Bruno now understands that revenge will be found in the long game. Eagerly investing in the new clockwork revolution, he builds his fortune and lays deep and subtle plans. Only his love for his blind sister Isabella and his desire to see her safe and married well tempers his coldly murderous purpose. Yet every morning, he sharpens the knife his uncle gave him and promises Angelina justice.

Your concept may also be used to create character Traits, along with those taken from the character's background and profession.

What's in a Name?

A character's name is written right at the top of their character sheet, but it can often be the last thing you think about when you are creating a new persona to play. Bear in mind that the character's name will be used a lot in the game, and may even say something about your character's image.

Typical Italian male given names end in -o or -e, or rarely -a or –i, whilst female given names tend to end in -a, and sometimes -e. There are 50 entries in each column, so a Guide can quickly conjure a new non-player character by randomly generating a number between 1 and 50 (perhaps using percentile dice and halving the roll) for first and last name.

EXAMPLE NAMES

	Female	Male	Surname
1	Adele	Alberto	Amato
2	Adriana	Alessandro	Barbieri
3	Agnese	Angelo	Bellini
4	Alessia	Antonio	Benedetti
5	Alice	Bernardo	Bernardi
6	Angela	Bruno	Bianchi
7	Anna	Carlo	Bruno
8	Arianna	Claudio	Caputo
9	Aurora	Daniele	Caruso
10	Beatrice	Dario	Castelli
11	Bettina	Davide	Cattaneo
12	Bianca	Domenico	Colombo
13	Carla	Emanuele	Coppola
14	Caterina	Enrico	Costa
15	Chiara	Enzo	D'Amico
16	Cristiana	Ercole	D'Angelo
17	Elisa	Ettore	De Luca
18	Fabrizia	Eugenio	De Rosa
19	Federica	Fabrizio	Esposito
20	Francesca	Federico	Fabbri
21	Gabriella	Filippo	Ferrara
22	Gaia	Flavio	Fontana
23	Gianna	Francesco	Franco
24	Giovanna	Franco	Galli
25	Giuliana	Gabriele	Gentile

EXAMPLE NAMES

	Female	Male	Surname
26	Giuseppina	Gennaro	Giordano
27	Ilaria	Gianni	Giuliani
28	Isabella	Giorgio	Grassi
29	Lucia	Giuliano	Leone
30	Lucrezia	Giuseppe	Lombardi
31	Luisa	Lorenzo	Longo
32	Maddalena	Luca	Mancini
33	Margerita	Luigi	Mariani
34	Maria	Marco	Marino
35	Martina	Mario	Martinelli
36	Massima	Massimo	Messina
37	Nicoletta	Matteo	Monti
38	Olivia	Maurizio	Moretti
39	Paola	Ottaviano	Neri
40	Patrizia	Paolo	Pellegrini
41	Rachele	Pietro	Ricci
42	Roberta	Riccardo	Rinaldi
43	Rosa	Roberto	Rizzo
44	Silvia	Salvatore	Romano
45	Simona	Silvio	Rossi
46	Sofia	Stefano	Russo
47	Stella	Tommaso	Serra
48	Teresa	Ulisse	Silvestri
49	Vittoria	Valentino	Valente
50	Viviana	Vittorio	Vitale

Age

You'll also find room on the character sheet to express your character's age. Starting player characters could be any age – however, if you play someone older, this can be reflected in their experience (p. 91). There is no need to put down an exact age; instead, add a phrase that describes something about how the character's age affects their behaviour or how they look. This phrase is likely to include Traits that you can optionally add to the character sheet, such as *Headstrong Youth, Mid-life Crisis, Young Mind in an Ageing Body,* or *Look Good for My Age.*

2. ATTRIBUTES

A player character has three Attributes: Body, Mind, and Soul. An Attribute is a core capability that is applied when facing Challenges. Traits are grouped within these Attributes:

- **Body** represents physical strength, endurance, and speed.
- **Mind** represents intellect, knowledge, and understanding.
- **Soul** represents sociability, resilience, emotional intelligence, and spirituality.

Starter player characters have a total of 9 points to spend across their Attributes. Attributes can have a maximum value of 5 to start with and a minimum of 1. Assume that a 2 means the Attribute is of a low-to-average level. As characters become more experienced, they will have the opportunity to increase the value of their Attributes.

Your choice of Attribute scores tells you something about your character. Selecting a value of 3 for each of Body, Mind, and Soul, would indicate a balanced and competent all-rounder. A character with values of 5, 2, 2 would be specialised and very strong in one area whilst just about average in the other two.

Your Attributes are always used directly in Challenges throughout the game. The value of the Attribute is the base number of dice to add into your pool, with other dice added from Traits. Attribute values are also used to measure how much damage or how many setbacks a character can take before they are knocked out of various types of Challenge.

Devorah Lazarus is happy that the new order in Florence means that even a Jew can be a clocker, and she is voraciously working her way through the volumes on her book wheel to be the best she can. But she is not so happy that she is averse to a little freelance work from time to time.

3. TRAITS AND MORE

There are three recommended ways to create characters:

i. Archetype

Starting on page 92 are a series of Archetypes, templates suited to the setting, from grizzled mercenary to struggling artist, each with sample Traits, Wealth levels, and suggested Goals, as well as a snapshot of their lives. They can then be modified by adding one of the Origins listed following the Archetypes. After all, a merchant from the maritime trading power of Venice will be different from one hailing from the banking capital of Milan. These provide a basis for final personalisation – add a name, at least a few sentences of backstory and character, set up to three Goals, and tweak the Traits to match the concept. Typically, you can add up to three new Traits at 3 or one at 5, or increase three existing Traits by 1 each. You can also, with the Guide's approval, modify Traits, whether in detail (*Classical Wrestling* could become *Knee to the Groin*) or in entirety (*Demure Daughter* to *Outspoken Widow*), and switch around the ratings given for each.

ii. Narrative

Start with a concept and description, however long or short, and use that as the basis for selecting 15 Traits, at least two in each of Body, Mind, and Soul, and at least one being a relationship. Of these:

- one Trait starts at 4d
- five Traits start at 3d
- five Traits start at 2d
- four Traits start at 1d

Wealth starts at 2d, but can be raised as high as 5d by swapping out dice from Traits. For example, a character could have Wealth 4d by reducing two 4d Traits to 3d. In addition, choose up to three Goals. For example, from the description of Bruno de Gasperi on page 82, we could derive the following:

Body Traits: *Enduring Limp 1d, Good with My Hands 1d, Sharp Knife 1d, Sleekly Elegant 2d*

Mind Traits: *Conceal Feelings 3d, Knows Florentine Mechanici 2d, Shrewd Banker 4d, Subtle Plans 2d*

Soul Traits: *Revenge on the Orsini 3d, Buried Anger 2d, Justice! 1d, Protective Love of Isabella 2d, Romantic Soul 2d, Take the Long View 2d, Big Name in Florentine Banking 2d*

Wealth: *5d*

As you can see, to get Wealth 5d, Bruno sacrifices three of his 3ds: one became a 2d and two became a 1d. These Traits include at least one relationship (Isabella – although one could also consider his connections with the mechanici of Florence as a relationship, too). This makes a good starting set of Traits, weaving story with abilities that will be used in play. We know where he is from, what he does, what is important to him, and where he is going.

iii. *Improvisation*

You can simply start with a name, a short concept, your Attributes, and a couple of particular Traits reflecting the character's notable strengths or experiences and take it from there, shaping the character as the game progresses. You can simply declare that the character has additional Traits in the course of the story, up to a maximum of nine (including any chosen during character creation):

- two Traits start at 4d
- three Traits start at 3d
- four Traits start at 2d

This approach is a trade-off, granting versatility in exchange for having a slightly smaller range of Traits. So, for example, Bruno might start as:

Florentine Banker 4d (Mind), Plans Revenge on the Orsini 4d (Soul), Blind Sister 3d (Soul)

The other Traits will manifest themselves in the course of play.

4. GOALS

Player characters typically have Goals they want to achieve. These are task-focused actions to be achieved in the game world as part of the story you are creating. Up to three Goals are noted on the character sheet, treated as Traits with values of 1–5d. They provide a guide to the player for directing the character's actions during play. The character will get a bonus when facing Challenges tightly bound to their Goals, or receive a penalty if initiating actions that run counter to them. You don't have to declare all three immediately when creating your character; often, Goals will emerge during play and they can be added at any time when you are populating your first three.

Goals can be grouped in a number of ways. A suggested array of goal types is:

1. A Long-term Goal that sits deeply in the heart of the character and could take several sessions or a lifetime to complete. Give it a value of 5d. *Example: Construct a clockwork horse that can win the Palio race in Siena.*

2. A Mid-term Goal shared with other members of the group that makes sense as a key driver within this particular adventure. Give it a value of 3d. *Example: Persuade Luigi to forgive my father's debts – the easy way or the hard way.*

3. A Short-term Goal directly related to the current story and game session. Give it a value of 1d. *Example: Be the first to get into Milady's bedchamber.*

When a Mid-term or Long-term Goal is successfully achieved, the player transfers it to a list of completed Goals on their character sheet. This will earn the character an immediate Minor Advancement (p. 158) and the player may choose a new Goal to replace the completed one. Short-term Goals do not give the same gain – but when one is completed, the player can immediately declare another there and then or wait for a future moment.

You can invoke Goals up to three times per game session. Short- and Mid-term Goals can be invoked multiple times in a session. A Long-term Goal can only be invoked once in a session, at a suitably pivotal moment. This gives you a bonus in a Challenge equal to the Goal's Trait value. An invoked Goal provides a benefit for one die roll. For further rules on Goals, including the consequences of failing a Challenge where you invoke one, see page 146.

Goals should focus on a clear outcome – an objective that can be achieved during the game through character action. *I want to be the best swordsman in all of Italy* is not focused enough: how can anyone know if they are the best anywhere? However, *Prove that I am the greatest swordsman in the world by besting Monsieur D'Orleans in a duel* is perfect, as it gives a clear measure of what success would look like and an objective bursting with story potential.

> **Example:** *Arabella is trying to trail a corrupt priest to the conspirators' meeting place without being spotted by his henchman. She chooses a Short-term Goal: 'Stay undercover'. As it is a Short-term Goal, it has a value of 1d. Arabella can now use the Goal for this scene and add it to her pool of dice. The Goal slot is emptied once she has been detected or has otherwise completed this phase of the session. Her player can then immediately choose another Goal or wait until an opportune one springs to mind.*

Samsone the Clockwork Dog is as extraordinary for its capabilities as for the fact that no one is sure who made it. A tightly-coiled spring slotted into its back will power this exquisitely crafted metal dog for hours. It can be set to patrol a set space randomly, barking at intruders and then, if that does not drive them away, attacking them. Alternatively, it can guard a gate, pull a cart, or even carry a message, running at almost 6 miles per hour.

Body 3, Mind 1, Soul 1. Good Dog +d, Metal Bite 3d. Metal Shell +2d, Metal Jaws +2d.

5. STARTING WEALTH

This is not a game in which it is important to pay too much attention to how many arrows are left in the hero's quiver or exactly which medicines are in the doctor's bag. Characters are assumed to have whatever equipment is indicated by their skills, profession, and lifestyle – the tools of their trade, weapons and armour, a horse, and so on. Particular items of note can be written on the character's sheet with the bonus dice they impart (p. 150); they are immediately available to the character and can be used in the story. Other items will need to be acquired during play. Use common sense – rarer or more specialist items will be harder to acquire (or require Wealth or similar checks), and the Guide may rule that certain items are harder to find. A character generally has access to food, for example, but even a rich one might find it tricky to host a lavish banquet in the middle of a city that is starving during a five-month siege.

Equipment has a value associated with it, just like Attributes and Traits. One piece of equipment can be added to the pool of dice if that makes sense in the context of a Challenge. Not everything needs numbers, though, only those most likely to be used or least obvious in application. If needs be, the Guide can always assign bonuses on the fly.

Wealth is abstracted as a Trait, which can be used quickly to assess whether or not a character has the resources needed to acquire a particular item necessary for the story, and gives an overall feel for the character's standard of living. It is rated from one to twelve dice, reflecting purchasing power and assets owned, as well as creditworthiness and favours owed. A character with one die in wealth is the poorest of the poor, having to scratch a day-to-day living with minimal, old, and worn-out possessions, uncertain about where their next meal will come from.

See the Wealth rules on page 148 for more on this. Likewise, special pieces of equipment with particular, often unique, characteristics – from those with unusual practical uses to those that have emotional significance – will get a Trait rating, such as *My Father's Sword* 3d, *Clockwork Revolver* 4d or *Relic of St Bona* 5d (the patron saint of Pisa and pilgrims, by the way).

Wealth rises and falls. If Wealth is not a focus of the game, characters' initial levels can simply be maintained as a point of reference that tells you how easy it is for a character to gain new items during play. Acquiring items or living a lifestyle set at a greater level than your Wealth is difficult and may have consequences. Acquiring items is a type of Challenge and is covered in the main Equipment section (p. 150).

WEALTH LEVELS

Wealth	Who?	Lifestyle
1	The destitute, the poorest of the poor	Hand to mouth, day-by-day existence, no luxuries, increased likelihood of disease
2	The poor, rural peasants, unskilled city workers, common soldiers, apprentices	Basic, limited opportunities, a few inexpensive luxuries
3	Established townsfolk, successful farmers, experienced mercenaries	Reasonable standard of living, perhaps with a simple house or town apartment, some luxuries
4	Successful artisans, the richest farmers, well-off merchants	Comfortable with a number of luxuries, larger and better accommodation, and continually improving prospects
5	Guildmasters, heads of minor aristocratic families	Very comfortable, used to regular luxuries and with enough surplus to maintain a large household and investments
6	Successful mercenary captains, bankers, bishops	Head of a substantial enterprise, living well and with ample funds

Above 6d, the difference is one of degree: how many servants and palaces you have; how easily can you raise an army (or get the loans needed to raise one) or commission great public works. A rating of 8d would fit the head of a great family, such as the Medici, Borgia, or Sforza; the Prince of Milan or the Doge of Venice are 9d; the King of France 10d; whilst 12d ratings are reserved for a handful of individuals in the world, such as the Pope (on a good day), the Holy Roman Emperor, and the Sultan of the Ottoman Empire.

6. FINISHING UP

Nudges

Nudges give a character a chance to tilt the odds in their favour (p. 142). A player character starts with 3 Nudges.

Experience

The default Trait levels suggest characters with a certain level of experience and competence. Rookie characters will generally have fewer Traits at lower levels. Conversely, more experienced characters may have a few more Traits with some at higher levels. An established hero might have a main Trait at 5d, for example, and three at 4d, whilst a legendary hero or arch-villain may have one defining Trait at 6d, and two or three others at 5d or 4d. Ultimately, the Guide is the arbiter. Of course, a trade-off might be lower Attributes, perhaps reflecting old wounds or the passage of time, or additional Flaws, such as impairments, onerous commitments, or blood enemies.

ARCHETYPES

Archetypes are basic 'packages' representing particular types of character in the world of *Gran Meccanismo*. Where Traits are listed in [square brackets], they denote a general class of Trait, and the specific Trait will depend on the particular character concept. For example, *[Reads Foreign Language]* could as easily be *Reads Latin* as *Reads French*, and *[Relationship to Patron]* can be whatever the player chooses – anything from *Resents Dependence on Master Franchi* to *Besotted Servant of the Widow Albizzi*. Feel free to modify them to fit the concept of the character.

The different archetypes' Traits add up to different totals. That is entirely deliberate, as it reflects the way that some Traits can be used more widely than others, and some backgrounds have specific advantages and drawbacks.

WHAT EVERYONE KNOWS

For the sake of convenience, it is assumed that everyone can speak Italian, although foreigners will speak it with a pronounced accent. This is not accurate – indeed, at the time, most Italians actually spoke regional dialects and variations of the language that many others could not understand – but it is a minor liberty that helps the game flow. That said, literacy is not the norm, and only characters with a relevant Trait can read and write.

THE ARTIFICER

"Roberto il costruttore, can you build it?"
"Yes, I can."

Maybe you are one of the *mechanici* [meh-KA-nee-chee], the new generation of Florentine technologists driving the clockpunk revolution, exploring new realms of water-clock-powered cogent engines, spring-driven carriages, and organ guns. But there are plenty of others who also build and invent, from the craftspeople who make the fine clockwork toys that grace the halls of the rich to the siege engineers who build or break elaborate fortifications or every kind. Not all Artificers are at the bleeding edge of the New Science, but then again, not everyone wants to bleed for their craft. Either way, all Artificers share not only a fascination with gadgets but also the principles behind them, not to mention the need for funds or a patron to keep them fed, housed, and in parts and labour.

Body Traits: Draughtsman 2d, Fine Manipulation 2d, Heedless of Appearance *or* Dressed for Success 2d
Mind Traits: [Builds Gadgets or Similar Professional Skill] 4d, Knows Scientific Principles 4d, Can Read and Write 2d
Soul Traits: [Relationship to Patron *or* Master] 2d, Fascinated by Science 3d, Focus 1d, Natural Salesperson *or* What Happens if I Do This? 1d
Wealth: 2d
Typical Goals: Finally perfect the flying clockwork chaffinch; Learn the secrets of Pirelli of Mantua; Acquire a copy of Hasan al-Rammah's *The Book of Military Horsemanship and Ingenious War Devices.*
Typical Equipment: Small Knife (+1d), Tools of the Trade (+2d), possibly a workshop, maybe a donkey to help carry raw materials and finished works, paper, pens, and lots of half-finished sketches and diagrams.

Variations

- The **Military Engineer** swaps the appearance-related Body Trait for *Experienced Campaigner.*
- The **Alchemist** is a chemist, whose professional skill is *Chemistry*, and who acquires the Body Trait of *Strange Smells* 2d.
- The **Venetian Glassblower** is a highly trained and equally highly prized specialist, whose defection from Venetian service triggers a manhunt and even a price on her head. She acquires *Glassblowing* 5d as a Mind Trait and the Soul Traits *Hunted by the Venetian Inquisition* 2d and *Paranoid* 2d.
- The **Clocker** is a hydronetic hacker of the water-clock computer, with the professional skill *Clocker* and just a single Soul Trait, *Obsessed with the New Science* 6d, replacing all those of the standard Artificer.

THE ARTISAN

"Yeah, I can make that. But it's a tricky job. Gonna cost you."

When it comes down to it, everything and everyone depends on you. The artists, the inventors, the doctors – how many of them know how to make their tools? The noblemen and the generals cut a fine figure, but who makes the weapons for their soldiers and builds them their palaces and castles? Some Artisans may be members of a guild, have a workshop with apprentices, but most just have a little shop or a stall in the market. When it comes down to it, you're one of the unsung heroes, proud of your skills but knowing full well that there is more to life than just a job.

Body Traits: Good with My Hands 3d, Work All Day 2d
Mind Traits: [Artisanal Skill] 4d, Creative 2d, Sell My Own Wares 2d
Soul Traits: [Relationship to Guild, Patron, *or* Master] 2d, Hard Worker 1d, Proud of My Work 2d
Wealth: 2d
Typical Goals: Woo and marry Sofia, the butcher's daughter; Become a guild master; Find a way to get the prince himself to use my plates, proving once and for all that I am a better potter than my awful brother-in-law, Ernesto.
Typical Equipment: Small, Sharp Knife (+1d), Tools of the Trade (+2d), small workshop or market stall.

Guilds

In the cities, it is pretty much mandatory for Artisans to be a member of a guild. These associations have both a social and a religious dimension – they hold feasts on their patron saints' days, provide support for members' widows and the like – but, above all, they set the rules for all business done in their field and territory. It is the guilds that control entry into the business, limit outside competition, govern the treatment and training of apprentices, and otherwise establish the standards of quality and behaviour. In Florence, for example, the main ones are the Guild of Doctors and Specialists (not just for doctors, but also apothecaries, spice merchants, and toolmakers of every kind), the Guild of Silk (primarily silk workers, but also goldsmiths, as they produce gold thread), the Guild of Masters of Stone and Wood (carpenters, sculptors, architects) and the Company of St Luke (artists).

THE ARTIST

"This is great art ~ my art. However, I have discovered that few understand the true depths of my genius."

Art is more than just beauty. In these times, it is a mark of power and wealth, and if you get to be good enough, you'll have rich patrons eager for your services. It is also part of the New Science – the line between artist, philosopher, engineer, and architect is often a fine one, as da Vinci himself has shown.

Like Artisans, successful Artists often establish their own workshops, with accompanying apprentices, acolytes, students, servants, and hangers-on. Sometimes well-to-do parents or young men will pay for lessons; at other times the apprentices work on their master's great art. For example, the master might sketch in the outlines of a fresco and concentrate on the detail, whilst the students paint in the sky and background.

Body Traits: Eye for Detail 1d
Mind Traits: Knows the Art Business 1d, Painter *or* Sculptor 3d
Soul Traits: [Relationship to Patron, Teacher *or* Apprentice] 2d, Art for Art's Sake 2d, Confident in My Abilities *or* Tortured Genius 2d, Inspiration 3d
Wealth: 2d
Typical Goals: Find the perfect sky-blue pigment; Have Isabella d'Este commission me to paint her portrait; Set up my own workshop.
Typical Equipment: Brushes, paper, chisels, or other Tools of the Art (+1d), flagon of cheap wine, room in a master's workshop, or own studio (maybe even own workshop).

MICHELANGELO, 'IL DIVINO'

Michelangelo di Lodovico Buonarroti Simoni is one of the giants of the age – painter, sculptor, and architect. Impassioned and impetuous, he is at present, aged 35, in the service of the Vatican, building the Papal Tomb and painting an extraordinary scene across the ceiling of the Sistine Chapel. Michelangelo is not especially interested in fine living or even a comfortable life. He lives simply, his manners are rough, and his passion reserved largely for his art. A devout Catholic, however, he is horrified by the New Science, and has vowed never to return to his native Florence whilst it is in the grips of this heresy.

Body 3, Mind 2, Soul 5. Inspirational Artist 10d, Dramatic Sculptor 10d, Fine Architect 8d, Famous across Italy 8d, Simple Life 4d, Slave to His Art 5d, Foe of the New Science 5d

Corrado Sacchi, head of his family's bank, often claims that he has heard every crackpot scheme and dubious excuse under the sun, but sometimes even he can be surprised.

THE BANKER

"These numbers are more than tallies of profit and loss. Behind them are tales of foolishness and thrift, adventure and security, risk and reward. And I hold the ledger."

This is an age when banking has suddenly emerged as a major force behind international trade, speculative entrepreneurship, and the business of statecraft. Shopkeepers, priests, and kings all need the services of Bankers such as you, and times are good.

Body Traits: Enjoys the Good Life 2d
Mind Traits: Head for Business 2d, Financial Machinations 2d, Numerate 3d, Can Read and Write Latin 1d
Soul Traits: Love of Money *or* Money Is Power 2d, [Relationship to Patron *or* Agent] 2d
Wealth: 4d
Typical Goals: Set up my own private bank; Commission Titian to paint my portrait; Marry into the aristocracy.
Typical Equipment: Fine Clothes (+2d), town house, horse, servant, ledgers, paper, and pens.

THE BRAVO

"Are you looking at me, ser? Stand aside lest I carve you like the Sunday roast!"

You are an entrepreneur of violence. Maybe you're just a hired thug, a bruiser from the rough part of town, or maybe you pretend to dandyish sophistication, but no matter how you choose to comport yourself, your business is menace and murder. In these rough times, that means you get a lot of business, whether as an assassin or a bodyguard.

Down on your luck, you may become a soldier or a bandit, or you may simply work from contract to contract, threatening a defaulting debtor for his banker here, disposing of an indiscreet ex-lover there; but, like most Bravos, you generally aspire to a position within an aristocrat's household. That's the good life; occasionally you'll need to get your blade bloody, but most of the time you can loll around cadging food from the kitchens and eyeing up the servant girls, except when it's time to accompany one of the family to church, business, or social engagements and look tough.

Body Traits: Murderous Swordsman 2d, Quick with a Knife 3d, Swaggering Bravado 3d
Mind Traits: Knows the Local Backstreets 2d
Soul Traits: [Relationship to Patron *or* Partner] 1d, Killer 2d
Wealth: 2d
Typical Goals: Become the duke's right-hand man; Kill my rival Grimaldi and take his woman for myself; Make enough money to be able to get out of this business.
Typical Equipment: Knife (+1d), Sword (+2d), Flashy Clothes (+1d), Leather Jerkin (+1d).

Variations

- The **Poisoner** is a specialised assassin, who replaces *Murderous Swordsman* and *Swaggering Bravado* with the Mind Trait *Knows Poisons* 3d and the Soul Trait *Subtle Schemer* 1d.
- Given the risks that deter many from the duty, the small corps of Florentine **Glider Pilots** are drawn heavily from free-spirited Bravos, and they replace the Body Trait Murderous Swordsman with the Traits *Glider Pilot* 2d and *Light Frame* 2d, swap *Killer* for *Adrenaline Junky* 2d, and swap *Knows the Local Backstreets* for *Navigate from the Air* 2d.

THE DOCTOR

"This is going to hurt."

You are a member of the educated elite. You went to one of the great universities, maybe Padua or Bologna. You studied for ten years to become a Doctor of Medicine. You understand that many ills are caused by imbalances in the patient's humours (p. 58) and can try to rectify that by feeding them herbs and potions or by bleeding them with leeches. You have a grasp of anatomy and may even have heard Fracastoro's new-fangled idea that some diseases are infections from outside sources. However, for all that, your cures often come down to guesswork, prayer, and the quickest amputations you can manage.

Body Traits: Swift Amputation 1d, Sensitive Fingers 2d, Strong Stomach 2d
Mind Traits: Classical Education 2d, Diagnose Illness 2d, First Aid 3d, Herbalism 2d, Can Read and Write Latin 2d
Soul Traits: Arrogant *or* Put My Patients at Ease 2d
Wealth: 3d
Typical Goals: Find just the right tincture of mercury to cure the pox; Buy myself a fine summer house in the country; Avoid having to go and inspect that ship's crew for signs of the Plague.
Typical Equipment: Probes, saws, a magnifying glass and other Doctor's Implements (+2d), Fine Clothes (+2d), Notebooks of Anatomical Studies (+1d), small house in town with consulting room, maybe a servant.

ASSASSINIO!

Murder for hire is common, and whilst most assassins are just backstreet thugs or common servants, that doesn't mean the law treats this crime lightly. The men who murdered two Bolognese aristocrats in Florence, for example, were paraded through the streets to the square where they committed the crime, their right hands were cut off, and then they were hanged, their bodies hacked apart and then burned outside the city walls. The locals who had sheltered and assisted them were exiled to the barren island of Elba and their houses were destroyed in a symbolic act giving them no remaining place in the city. The moral of this story? Don't get caught.

THE ENTERTAINER

"Gather round, friends, and prepare to be transported, delighted, educated, and enlightened, and all for the price of a simple meal and perhaps a jar of wine!"

Everyone likes to be diverted, and that's where you come in. You may be a singer or a storyteller, a musician or an actor, but it's all about entertaining your audience. Of course, this is often a life on the road, so you may well also have some other sideline, which could be something wholly legal, such as mending shoes or sketching portraits, to something less so, like pickpocketing or a little light espionage.

Body Traits: Brawl 1d, Compelling Voice *or* Charismatic Presence *or* Looks the Part 3d, Recognisable Looks 2d, [Day Job Skill] 1d
Mind Traits: Can Read Music *or* Can Read and Write 2d, Memory for a Script *or* Plays [Instrument] *or* Talented Singer 2d
Soul Traits: Party Hard 2d, Plays to the Audience 1d
Wealth: 2d
Typical Goals: Get to play in the d'Este court and win a patron; Assemble my own troupe so I don't have to act any more; Use the performance to catch the eye of that charming young noble in the front row.
Typical Equipment: Flamboyant Clothes (+1d), Musical Instrument or other necessary Tool of the Trade (+2d).

Variations

- This is the profile of a moderately successful professional entertainer. There is also the **Troupe Manager**, who runs their own little band of actors or musicians and will also have the Mind Trait *Runs a Business* 2d and the Soul Trait *Worries about the Next Contract* 2d.

Instruments of Renaissance Italy

There is a wide range of instruments in use, although the voice is still seen as the most important. These include the droning, cranked hurdy-gurdy, the guitar-like lute, the simple trumpet, drums, the tambourine, the harpsichord (an early piano), and pipes, like the shawm and the recorder.

THE FARMER

"You want to eat, you got to work"

When it comes down to it, without Farmers, nothing else works. You may be raising cattle for their milk, ploughing fields with an ox, or cultivating vines or olive groves, but this hard work is what keeps everyone fed.

Body Traits: Endures the Elements 2d, Hours of Toil 3d, Strong Back 3d, Wrestling 1d

Mind Traits: Animal Lore 1d, Knows Farming 2d

Soul Traits: [Relationship to Family] 3d, Earthy Sense of Humour 1d, Salt of the Earth 2d

Wealth: 1d

Typical Goals: See one of my sons join the clergy and get out of this life; Finally end the generations-long vendetta with the Grimaldis on the other side of the rise; Buy a second ox.

Typical Equipment: Hut or small house on smallholding, maybe an ox or a horse.

THE MERCHANT

"These are exciting times for an entrepreneur with a nose for business, an eye for a deal, and the nerve to take risks. Someone, in short, like me."

There has always been a place for the travelling Merchant or the market trader, but with new commercial routes opening up and bringing in goods from across the Atlantic Ocean to the west and beyond the Ottoman Empire to the east, business is booming.

Body Traits: Works Long Hours 1d
Mind Traits: Basic Economics 3d, Can Evaluate Goods 3d, Sales Patter 2d
Soul Traits: [Relationship with Guild, Banker, Supplier, *or* Client] 2d, Greedy 1d, Can Weigh up a Client 1d
Wealth: 4d
Typical Goals: Pay off my loan from the Gondis before the interest sucks me dry; Persuade my daughter to follow me into the family business; Get the backing to launch a trade expedition to distant Muscovy.
Typical Equipment: Trade goods, a shop, market stall, or wagon, a strong lock-box, an apprentice, waggoneer, guard, or servant.

Variations

- A settled **Shopkeeper** might have more or stronger relationships with the local community and *Can Spot a Shoplifter* 2d, but only 3d Wealth.

THE NE'ER-DO-WELL

"Look, I can explain!"

In the towns, you may be a thief, a con artist, a beggar, a cutthroat, or a burglar. In the countryside, you're a bandit, a sheep-rustler, a horse-thief, or a wandering fraud pretending to be a monk or a fortune-teller for a meal, a bed, and a chance to abscond with whatever strikes your fancy before anyone else is awake. A shame the money never lasts for long, the girl leaves you, and the trinkets turn out to be worthless. Maybe it's not your fault and you're just down on your luck, or maybe you're just a bad 'un through and through. Either way, you rely on your wits, a quick smile, and, if all else fails, a sharp knife and a clean pair of heels.

Body Traits: Honest Face 1d, Can Outrun Any Pursuer 2d, Unexpected Knife to the Ribs 2d
Mind Traits: Know My Way Around 4d, Plausible Story 2d, Quick Wits 3d
Soul Traits: Feels No Guilt 3d, Scrounger 2d
Wealth: 1d
Typical Goals: Have my revenge; Find a wife and a place to start a new life; Convince the village that I am the duke's tax collector.
Typical Equipment: Knife (+1d).

Variations

- For a **Victim of Circumstance**, add a Trait at 2d that reflects the character's past life and profession, or else the sad past that set them down on their luck. Anything from *Once an Honest Potter* to *Sudden Temper*.
- For the real **Bandit**, instead of *Honest Face* and *Can Outrun Any Pursuer*, the Traits *Villainous Looks* and *Sudden Ambush* are more appropriate, as well as *Archery* 2d or some other weapon skill.

THE NOBLEMAN

"Blood is thicker than water. And as easily spilled."

Despite the power of the Church and the rise of the new middle class, the bankers and the Florentine mechanici, this is still an aristocratic age when power is held by the noble families, greater and lesser. You might wear silks and enjoy the finer things in life – but, ultimately, you survive because you are willing to do whatever it takes to maintain your power, and will not go quietly.

Body Traits: Elegant Duellist 1d, Formal Dance 2d, Snobbish Poise 2d, Horse Rider 2d
Mind Traits: Classical Education 3d, Etiquette 3d, Noble Entertainments 2d, Political Savvy 1d
Soul Traits: [Relationship with Family] 3d, Sense of Superiority 2d
Wealth: 5d
Typical Goals: Marry the unpleasant Isabella Bentivoglio for her generous dowry; Persuade my father to give me a castle, even if it's just an itty-bitty one; Sneak away from the reception for the new cardinal with my blue-blood friends for a night on the town.
Typical Equipment: Sumptuous Clothes (+2d), a horse or carriage, Finely-crafted Duelling Sword (+2d), elegant house or rooms in parents' villa, servants and hangers-on.

Variations

- Not every Nobleman is a political animal; a more self-indulgent **Dilettante** might sacrifice *Duellist* and *Political Sense* for the Body Trait *Carouse All Night* 2d, the Mind Trait *Biting Wit* 2d, and the Soul Trait *Spoilt Fop* 2d.
- It was certainly not unknown for an aristocrat to raise his **Illegitimate Son** in his household and, although he would generally never inherit full rank and title, such a son could still enjoy life, albeit with the Flaw *Illegitimate and Disinherited Son* 4d and possibly other Soul Traits to match, whether *Secret Resentments* or *Grateful for What I have.*

THE NOBLEWOMAN

"I am, of course, my lord's obedient daughter."

The traditional role of the Noblewoman was to be a tool of dynastic survival and household management – to be married off advantageously at an early age, to bear male heirs and to keep her husband happy and his estates in good order. However, this is a time of change and everywhere there are those who are challenging old restraints, with women governing city states (even if usually as regents for young heirs), holding salons at which artists, poets, and philosophers share wine and wisdom, and even writing, thinking, and taking lovers openly, as if they were men!

Body Traits: Elegant Manner 2d, Formal Dance 2d, Horse Rider 1d, Talented Singer *or* Plays [Instrument] *or* [Some Other 'Womanly Accomplishment'] 2d
Mind Traits: Domestic Manager 3d, Etiquette 3d, Noble Entertainments 2d, Observant 2d
Soul Traits: [Relationship to Father *or* Husband] 3d, Sense of Duty 2d
Wealth: 3d
Typical Goals: Manage to avoid being betrothed to that ghastly Malatesta boy; Find some way to sneak that handsome stable boy into my rooms tonight; Convince Vittoria Colonna to attend my salon and impress her with my writing.
Typical Equipment: Sumptuous Clothes (+2d), horse or carriage, elegant house or rooms in parents' or husband's villa, servants and hangers-on.

Variations

- The **Courtesan** may not be of noble birth, but she knows how to ape the ways of the aristocracy as she hunts for a powerful husband, or simply monetises the appetites of her clients. Her Wealth will be just 2d, her Soul Traits will be *[Relationship to Patron]* 2d and *Love Them and Leave Them* 2d, and she will have one of the Body Traits *Arts of Love* 2d or *Look My Best* 2d, or else the Mind Trait *Perceive Desires* 2d.

THE PRIEST

"Dominus vobiscum!"

May the Lord be with you! Maybe you were called to the clergy and have devoted yourself to protecting the spiritual health of your flock, whether by wise counsel or through ruthlessly suppressing the heretics, schismatics, witches, and devil-worshippers who might seduce them from the path to heaven. But it could just as easily be that you ended up wearing the robes of a Catholic clergyman or monk because your family had no other use for you. Faith is power, though, and the local Priest is an authority in his own village, just as the bishops and cardinals are spiritual lords across the land.

Body Traits: Commanding Voice 1d, Raise up Your Voice Unto the Lord 1d

Mind Traits: Catholic Catechism 4d, Church Politics 3d, Knows Latin 3d, Can Read and Write 2d

Soul Traits: [Relationship to Congregation] 3d, [Relationship to Spiritual Superior] 2d, Devoted Christian 3d, Can Sniff out Sin 1d

Wealth: 2d

Typical Goals: Found and build my own church; Uncover the coven of devil-worshippers I am sure were behind the poor harvest; Not have a single impure thought from sunrise to sundown.

Typical Equipment: Simple Cassock (+0d) through to Sumptuous Robes (+3d) depending on rank, Bible (+1d).

Variations

- A **Monk** or **Nun** might have *Silent Prayer* and *Endure Hardships* instead of a *Commanding Voice* or a relationship with a congregation. As Monks' and Nuns' communities also had to fend for themselves in the main, both would generally also have one practical skill at 2d, such as *Woodcutter*, *Herbalist*, *Brewer*, or *Simple Tailor*. Given their vows of poverty, a Monk or Nun has Wealth 1d.

- An **Inquisitor** from the Dominican Order, on the other hand, might well replace *Raise up Your Voice Unto the Lord* with *Torture in God's Name* as a Body, Mind, or Soul Trait, depending on their preferred techniques.

THE RABBLE-ROUSER

"Can you hear it coming? Can you hear it, between the ticks and tocks of the clockwork, between the Ave Marias of the priests, between the groans of the suffering masses? That is the sound of change, my friend, the whisper of revolution!"

This is a time when all the old certainties are being brought into question, when everything from religious doctrine to artistic conventions is open to negotiation. For many, that is a terrifying thought, but for someone like you it is an intoxicating prospect, and in your cause you have found something to believe in, something that has turned your life upside down. You may be a cynical demagogue who sees a chance to win power and money, or a wide-eyed idealist eager to play the midwife to a better world, or maybe even a ruthless revolutionary willing to use the most violent of means in pursuit of a beautiful end – but whatever your true motivations, you know you will change the world.

Body Traits: Enthusiastic Brawler *or* Dart out of Sight 2d, Living on a Shoestring 2d, Penetrating Voice 1d
Mind Traits: Knows [Belief *or* Cause] 3d, Inky-fingered Printer *or* Sneaky Satirist *or* Passionate Orator 2d, Can Read and Write 1d
Soul Traits: Believer in the Cause 4d, Inspiring Leader *or* Cunning Schemer 2d, [Relationship to Group, Leader, Follower, *or* Ally] 2d
Wealth: 1d
Typical Goals: Root the Inquisition out of Florence once and for all; Set up a cell of the Movement amongst the students of Milan; Uncover the agent provocateur who has infiltrated the Movement.
Typical Equipment: Handful of cheaply-printed leaflets, notebook, charcoal, Hidden Knife (+1d).

Variations

- The Rabble-rouser may be an **Aristocratic Black Sheep**, in which case *Living on a Shoestring* is replaced with the Soul Traits *Class Traitor* 2d and *Estranged Family* 3d.
- The **Agent Provocateur** swaps *Believer in the Cause* 4d with the Soul Traits *Dangerous Secret* 4d and *Two-faced* 3d, and swaps *Living on a Shoestring* 2d with the Mind Trait *Undercover Tradecraft* 1d.
- A more **Violent Revolutionary** might add the Body Trait *Knifeman* 2d or the Mind Trait *Improvised Explosive* 2d, as well as *Wanted by [Specific City or Group]* 2d.

THE SAILOR

"Oh, I've seen sights. Mermaids off Gibraltar's rocks, the Venetian fleet at sail, Leviathan stirring beneath the Aegean."

The Mediterranean is part and parcel of the Italian legacy, and these days its explorers, such as Caboto and Columbus, range across the oceans wide. Sailors such as you, whether merchant seamen or fishermen, are crucial to the economy and just as necessary in times of war.

Body Traits: Agile 1d, Brawler 2d, Drinks Like a Fish 2d, Knife in My Boot 2d, Rower 1d, Strong Swimmer 3d
Mind Traits: Can Navigate by the Stars 1d, Can Predict the Weather 1d, Sea Lore 2d
Soul Traits: [Relationship with Shipmates] 3d, Lives for Today 2d, Superstitious 2d
Wealth: 2d
Typical Goals: Save up enough to get off this ship and set up a little dockside wine-shop (I'd rather listen to tales of life on the sea than keep living it); In some storm, have my secret revenge on Beppo the bosun; Finally make it to Constantinople.
Typical Equipment: Knife (+1d), assorted maps or shipping logs, trinkets from distant ports.

Variations

- The line between Sailor and **Pirate** is a fine one, and the distinction often depends on the opportunities and whether or not the other ship is of a different faith or nation. Although Venice has a treaty with the Ottoman Empire, for example, many other Christian ships treat Muslim vessels as fair game. A Pirate might have a more serious weapon instead of a knife and a Trait to match, as well as a Soul Trait such as *Bloodthirsty* or *Greedy* 2d.

THE SCHOLAR

"Blinding ignorance misleads us. Oh, wretched souls, open your eyes!"

This is a time of knowledge: its discovery, rediscovery, production, and transmission. Scholars such as you are not just professors and experimenters; they are also teachers, bookkeepers, lawyers, and administrators. Some are held in the highest esteem, called *dottore* (doctor) and *magister* (master), and provided with generous stipends by noble patrons eager to seem cultured or looking for a favourable reference in their next book. Others are down-at-heel clerks or forced to tutor (or at least try to tutor) spoiled rich kids in Latin for a few coins and an occasional free meal.

Body Traits: Lecturer's Voice 1d, Scrawny and Pallid 1d, Can Study Through the Night 1d

Mind Traits: Knows Latin 3d, Phenomenal Memory 2d, Can Read and Write 3d, Knows [Specialist Field] 4d, Relationship to [Mentor, Student *or* Institution] 1d, Tedious Explication 2d

Soul Traits: Curious Mind 2d, Intellectual Snob *or* Charismatic Teacher 2d

Wealth: 2d

Typical Goals: To be hired onto the faculty of Bologna University; To get my hands on the Brass Head of Pope Sylvester II (p. 21); To show up that bully, Captain Bonaventura, for the way he treated me the other day.

Typical Equipment: Impressive but worn Church or University Robes (+1d), books, parchment, and pens.

Variations

- The **Church Scholar** pores over scripture and canon law, replacing *Curious Mind* with *Church Politics*.
- The **Lawyer** replaces *Lecturer's Voice* with the Mind Trait *Cunning Argumentation* and swaps *Curious Mind* for *The Law Is What I Say It Is*.
- The **Secretary**, **Scrivener**, or **Accountant** replaces *Lecturer's Voice* with the Mind Traits *Know My Master's Secrets*, *Fine Penmanship*, or *Mathematics*, respectively. In each case, the specialist field is appropriate to their profession.

The modern warrior of 1510 must come to terms with the new realities of war. As a successful condottiere, Giovanni da Verona wears the heavy plate mail that is as much a mark of wealth as a source of protection, but he has also invested in the latest hand-crafted revolver from Florence – itself an expensive indulgence.

THE SOLDIER

"I kills people. That's what I does, and that's what I'm good at."

This is a time of war, so there's always work, blood, and plunder for someone like you with a talent for this trade. Some cities, like Florence and Venice, raise their own armies the way the French and Spanish do. Most still hire mercenaries on a *condotta* (contract). But when it comes down to it, everyone on the battlefield is bought and paid for by someone, right?

Body Traits: [Weapon of Choice] 3d, [Secondary Weapon] 1d, Duck and Cover *or* Fights Dirty 2d, Experienced Marcher 1d, Muscular 2d

Mind Traits: Cunning Tactics 2d, Can Evaluate Loot 1d, [Specialist Talent or Job, such as Barrack-room Lawyer, First Aid or Quartermaster] 1d

Soul Traits: Bloodlust *or* Coward *or* Just Following Orders *or* Once More Unto the Breach! 2d, Loyal to My Comrades 2d

Wealth: 3d

Typical Goals: Get through this campaign alive and retire; Gather enough plunder and glory to establish myself as a commander; Find a safe moment to kill that pig, Captain Bonaventura.

Typical Equipment: Average-quality weapons, Light Mail Armour (+2d).

Variations

- The **Cavalryman** replaces *Experienced Marcher* with *Horse Rider*.
- The **Artilleryman** reduces his main weapon skill to 1d and adds the Mind Trait *Gunnery* or *Siege Warfare* 2d (or 3d with the Flaw *Partially Deaf* 2d).
- The **Captain** replaces *Experienced Marcher* with *Horse Rider*, *Cunning Tactics* with *Battlefield Strategy*, and *Loyal to My Mates* with *[Relationship to Patron, Commander, or Unit]*, and adds *Voice of Command* 2d.

THE SPY

"The name's Bondi. Giacomo Bondi."

Intrigue flows in your veins, and your wits are as sharp as the knife at your belt – and the other ones hidden in your boot, purse, and mattress. Whether you are a freelancer or in the employ of one of the greater families or cities, this is an age of plot and subterfuge, where information is gold and you're the banker.

Body Traits: Keen Eye 2d, Quick Knife 3d, Horse Rider 2d
Mind Traits: Good Memory 1d, Ear for Gossip 2d, Nose for Politics 2d, Sharp Wits 3d, Street Smart 1d
Soul Traits: [Relationship to Patron] *or* Out for Myself 3d, Smooth Liar 2d
Wealth: 3d
Typical Goals: Find a way to access the secrets of Florence's Gran Meccanismo; Infiltrate the personal household of Cardinal Pazzi; Steal back that incriminating document that keeps me working for the tyrant of Parma.
Typical Equipment: Notebook, Stiletto Knife (+1d), horse.

Variations

- Some city-states have their own **Investigators**, such as the Venetian Inquisition or the magistrates of Florence and Milan. They swap *Smooth Liar* 2d for the Mind Traits *Knows the Law* 2d and *Criminal Investigator* 2d. They might also have a Soul Trait, such as *The Truth is Out There* 2d or *Agent of Justice* 2d.

BALDASSARE CASTIGLIONI, THE CONSUMMATE COURTIER

Diplomat, author, and soldier, Castiglioni [Cas-till-lee-OH-nee] is perhaps best known for his *Book of the Courtier*, the handy how-to guide on the court etiquette and morality of the age. He spends much of his time at the court in Urbino, but travels widely – his wit, learning, and elegance making him welcome all across Italy. What better cover for one of the Vatican's most cunning and perceptive spies? His capacity to get priests and princes alike to tell him their innermost thoughts is not to be underestimated.

Body 1, Mind 5, Soul 4. Everyone Talks to Me 6d, Impeccable Manners 7d, Rapier Wit 5d, Dressed Just So 5d

THE WOODSMAN

"Mmf."

You may be a hunter, a bandit, a logger, or a charcoal burner. To tell the truth, you've probably been all of them at one point or another, as well as anything else that helps keep body and soul together.

Body Traits: Dirty Woodsman 3d, Muscular 3d, Can Swing an Axe 2d, Woodland Senses 2d
Mind Traits: Canny 1d, Knows the Ways of the Woods 2d, Trapper 3d
Soul Traits: Awkward in Company 2d, Close-lipped 3d, Loner 1d, Survivor 4d
Wealth: 1d
Typical Goals: Find a wife; Have revenge on the landlord who drove me from my farm and into the woods; Find out who I really am, based on the gold seal ring I was clutching when, as a babe, I was abandoned in a woodland clearing for a hunter to discover.
Typical Equipment: Axe (+2d), Rough Knife (+1d), or Crude Bow (+1d), Filthy Clothes (+0d), wooden hut, shaggy dog.

Variations

- The **Hunter** (whom unkind souls might think also doubles as the **Poacher**) will swap *Can Swing an Axe* for *Archer*.
- The **Charcoal Burner** works in a small gang or family out in the woods, cutting down trees and turning the wood into charcoal for fires and forges. It's an essential job but a dirty one, and these *carbonari* are typically treated as near-outcasts. They acquire the Body Trait *Blackened and Smoky* 3d, and they replace *Loner* with *No One Trusts the Carbonari* and swap *Trapper* for *Knows Charcoal*.

THE WORKMAN

"Aye, we'll get round to it when we can, sir, never you mind."

It's all very well talking about a new world across the Atlantic and a New Science in Florence, but people still want things built, broken, collected up, and taken away. That's where you come in. It's a hard life, but it is what it is. Of course, it doesn't mean you don't have your own thoughts and dreams – but no one would really credit it, would they?

Body Traits: Brawler 2d, Good with My Hands 1d, Labourer's Muscles 2d
Mind Traits: I Know Someone Who Knows Someone 2d, Street Smart 2d
Soul Traits: [Relationship to Boss] 1d, [Relationship to Family *or* Friends] 3d, Aspires to Better Things *or* I Make Do With What I've Got 2d, No One Notices Folk Like Us 2d
Wealth: 2d
Typical Goals: Have a son; Duck out of work this afternoon to watch the fist fights in the main square; Avenge myself on Bishop Rava for the way my brother was tortured as a heretic just because Rava's sister smiled at him.
Typical Equipment: Small Knife (+1d), Simple Clothes (+0d).

Variations

- The **Quarryman** digs out the blocks and sheets of fine marble that the likes of Michelangelo turn into statuary; he loses *Street Smart* 2d but has *Labourer's Muscles* 3d.

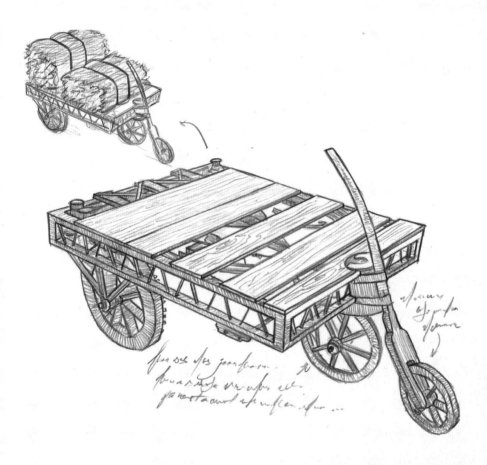

Da Vinci's revolutionary Mechanical Mule will follow a simple, pre-programmed route on its own, powered by coiled springs. It is increasingly used to move goods around warehouses and work sites, such as bales of wool or ores from a mine-head. Just make sure you don't get in its way. In the future, might the Mules even be unleashed in battle to ferry the wounded back from the front line — or to bring explosive charges into the midst of the enemy?

ORIGINS

These are additional modifiers a player may choose to add to an Archetype, largely related to where the character hails from. They offer a few notes and some additional Traits, at 1d unless otherwise noted. Where possible, roll the additional Traits into existing ones that seem appropriate. For example, if a character already has *Street Smart* 2d and comes from Rome, maybe *At Home in the Big City* will instead just add one die to *Street Smart*. But likewise, where a Trait doesn't fit the character concept, feel free to abandon or modify it. Also, if a character hails from a different part of Italy, or even abroad, you can assign a few minor Traits to reflect that. The location descriptions can also be mined for Traits, for that matter.

FLORENCE

"Let's try something different."

At this time, Florence is a place where tradition and accelerating modernity occasionally coexist, but frequently collide. Florentines are now widely regarded as entrepreneurial, unconventional, and often downright mad or subversive. You might just be another trader or condottiere looking for business, but outside Florentine lands you may find yourself persecuted as a threat to the national order, or followed around by curious locals expecting you suddenly to declaim some heretical new notion or pull out a marvel of the New Science simply because of your accent.

Extra Traits: Knows Florence, Unfazed by the New Science

GENOA

"What's out there?"

The Genoese are traders, explorers, and adventurers, as eager for a new adventure as for a good deal. They have a reputation for being a friendly and open-minded folk, up to the point when a deal is struck, and then they are as belligerent and intransigent as they come.

Extra Traits: Knows Genoa, Let's Make a Deal

KINGDOMS OF NAPLES AND SICILY

"That's the way it's always been done."

Subjects of the Spanish Crown, the southern Italians have been affected less by the intellectual and political ferment in the north, which is a good reason to stay put and a for some, good reason to get out for others.

Extra Traits: Knows the Sicilies, Knows [Home Town or Village]
Other Notes: Characters of aristocratic or official stock or position may also have the Mind Trait Can Speak Spanish.

MILAN

"I said I'd do it, didn't I?"

Milan is largely populated by Lombards, Italians of German descent, who are often that bit taller and heavier than their southern cousins, and sometimes still blond and blue-eyed. They are generally regarded as phlegmatic and hard-working, but also implacable once they make a decision. Whilst the Milanese rightly regard their city as Italy's true capital, other Italians tend to just consider them to be arrogant so-and-sos. Even so, if you want something done, often you'll want a Milanese.

Extra Traits: Knows Milan, Resents the French *or* Lackey of the French
Other Notes: It may be appropriate to grant a Body Trait, such as Hardy or Tall.

ROME

"We are Romans, the people of Empire!"

Romans have a reputation for being quick to anger, quick to violence, and quick to take advantage of any weakness. But, for all that, they do have a certain mystique because, well, Rome.

Extra Traits: Knows Rome, At Home in the Big City
Other Notes: Romans are infamous for packing knives. If the character doesn't already have some kind of weapon skills, then they also have Knife at the Ready 1d.

VENICE

"Ah, but there is something you didn't consider."

The Most Serene Republic's penchant for subterfuge and ruthless pragmatism are concealed behind a facade of sophisticated hedonism. The stereotypical Venetian is smarter, more ruthlessly subtle, probably richer, and certainly more decadent than you.

Extra Traits: Knows Venice, Strong Swimmer
Other Notes: Of course, not every Venetian is a crafty schemer, but if the character lacks any kind of similar Trait and it fits the character concept, add Cunning 1d.

JEW

"Yes, I'm a Jew. Why do you ask?"

As a minority frequently facing discrimination, Jews can hope to find some degree of freedom and opportunity in Italy, albeit with a yellow 'O' on their clothes.

Extra Traits: Knows [Home Town or Village], Jewish Faith, Mistrusted by Most Christians
Other Notes: Most Jews in Italy do not speak Hebrew, but if it fits the character concept, add it at 1d to 3d, depending on their proficiency. Alternatively, if they're a refugee from Spain, give them the Trait Can Speak Spanish.

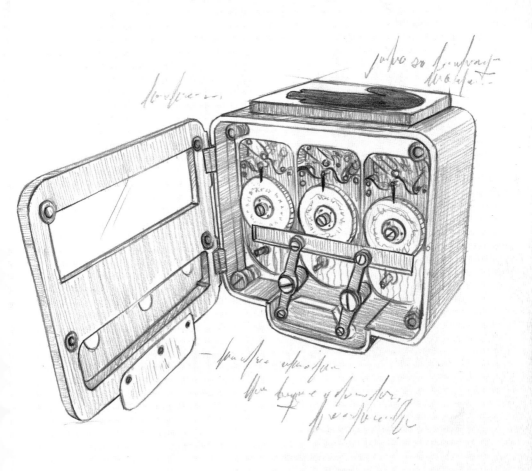

Although notoriously temperamental, the Palmlock promises to open only to the owner's handprint. Sadly, though, the owner doesn't still have to be attached to their hand.

Even murder can be stylish in Venice. The newly arrived consul for the Holy Roman Empire, Dieter von Heusenstamm from Frankfurt, should have known better than to carry his ciphers unescorted. Are his killers agents of Venice or the Vatican?

THE RULES

"Whoever arranges to found a Republic and establish rules in it, must presuppose that all men are bad and that they will use their malignity of mind every time they have the opportunity."

— Niccolò Machiavelli, *Discourses on Livy*

CHALLENGES

At the core of the *Gran Meccanismo* system are Challenges and their outcomes. Most of the time, especially when player characters are engaging in essentially mundane or risk-free activities with no real jeopardy to speak of, there's no need to roll dice. The players simply describe what their characters are doing and then it happens, subject to the Guide's interpretation. For example, a player states that their character goes to the market to stock up on provisions, for example and that's generally what happens in the game, nothing more to it. But what about if they spot a thief in the middle of the act and want to try to apprehend him in a hectic dash through the crowded marketplace? Or what if they find themselves face to face with the duke's henchmen, swords drawn? When matters become risky – to life and limb, to reputation, or simply to the players' plans – then the Challenges mechanic is there to resolve the outcome.

Here are some example challenges that your characters may face:

- Can your soldier face down the rioting mob and avoid a bloodbath?
- Will your scholar-investigator spot the traces of poison on the cardinal's wine goblet and thus be able to deduce that his death was a murder?
- Will your buffoon of a wastrel somehow be able to successfully engage a cynical official in a diverting conversation for more than fifteen minutes, giving friends time to 'borrow' the official's ledger?
- How successful will your mechanico be in building her revolutionary clockwork-powered pasta maker?
- How long can the small force of Genoese militiamen delay the advancing French army? Will it be enough time for the prince to escape?

These are key moments of uncertainty in the game – moments of tension when the outcome really matters and when there are real consequences of failure. As you can see from the examples, a Challenge could be set as a brief moment in time where an individual character is tested, or it could represent something that takes much longer and involves large numbers of people. Either way, whatever the scale of the moment in time, it is resolved essentially in the same way.

INITIATIVE

Many games have a step where you establish an order of action to manage the flow of the scene. In *Gran Meccanismo*, challenges arise naturally from the discussion around the table. It could be that, in the game dialogue, both a player character and an NPC are trying to achieve something quite different at the same time. The Guide reacts and responds to the action as it is described, setting Challenges as they emerge and making sense of the discussion, rather than having the scene operate according to a mechanically defined turn or initiative order.

This approach allows the sequence of events to flow. As the action starts to unfold, the Guide's main job is to ensure that the spotlight moves around the table, such that all the active participants and not just the most vocal of the group have opportunities, and to determine exactly what in the scene constitutes a Challenge. Active prompting and questioning can elicit a more organic sequencing of events with a little care and attention.

RESOLVING CHALLENGES

There are three ways that you can determine the outcome of a Challenge:

No-roll Challenges: Use these when you want to move on quickly and just need to check that a character has a high enough pool of dice to get past an obstacle.

One-roll Challenges: Use these when you want a quick resolution to a Challenge and want to start rolling dice.

Multi-roll Challenges: Use these when you want to take time getting into the detail of a Challenge – normally a complex or multi-part one. Different Attributes and Traits can be used over multiple dice rolls before a character wins.

NO-ROLL CHALLENGES

The simplest kind of Challenge is the No-roll Challenge, used for situations where you simply want to know whether there is a good chance something can be done, but you don't want to spend much time on it.

Here's a table with the number of successes you would expect on average from different sized pools of six-sided dice. The average number of successes is given with exacting Florentine precision, but the Guide can decide whether to round up or down in each situation, as they see fit.

NO-ROLL CHALLENGES

Number of Dice	Average Number of Successes
3	2
4	2.7
5	3.3
6	4
7	4.7
8	5.3
9	6
10	6.7
11	7.3
12	8
15	10
18	12
21	15

To resolve a No-roll Challenge, the player counts how many dice their character can use in the Challenge. Typically, this will be the relevant Attribute plus one Trait, possibly plus some equipment. See the next section for the complete rules for building a dice pool. The player doesn't need to collect the dice and roll them – they just tell the Guide how many dice they would have thrown.

The Guide will set a Difficulty number for the challenge (p. 125) and then check the average number of successes the player character would have achieved had the dice been rolled. They then compare this number to the Difficulty. If it is equal to or higher than the Difficulty, the Challenge is won. If lower, it is lost. See Outcomes (p. 134) for the consequences of such a defeat.

The procedure is very quick once you get used to it. Other forms of Challenge introduce the delicious uncertainty that comes with rolling handfuls of dice.

ONE-ROLL CHALLENGES

A One-roll Challenge is the main way to resolve action in the game. Both sides roll their dice pool and compare their results. Either party can initiate a Challenge. The Challenge is over in one roll, with the winner able to dictate the outcome based on the intent agreed before the roll.

To resolve a One-roll Challenge, go through the following steps:

1. Check intent and desired outcomes – what does each side want to accomplish?
2. The Guide sets the Difficulty or assembles the opposing dice pool for an adversary.
3. Select, or create, and share any applicable Scene Traits.
4. Build the player character's dice pool.
5. Roll the dice, add up the successes, and see who wins.
6. The winner gets their desired outcome.

Check Intent and Desired Outcomes

Sometimes, the effects of winning and losing a Challenge will be obvious when it is set up. Sometimes, one or the other will be less clear, in which case things need to be declared up front and the stakes for defeat set out. This is frequently the case for Challenges involving social Traits.

If the parties involved want different things from the Challenge, it may be time to break it into two or more separate Challenges and go through the process separately for each.

It's always useful to decide whether a Challenge is based on Body, Mind, or Soul. This is often obvious, but if not, whoever initiates the Challenge decides. It is entirely possible for the two sides to be using different Attributes; for example, someone could be trying to draw on their courage (Soul) to resist being intimidated by a bully showing off their muscular bulk (Body), or their wit (Mind) or talk their way past them.

The desired objective is achieved by the winner of the Challenge; however, it is possible to modulate the result depending on how much you beat the opposition, as explained in the Outcomes section (p. 134).

Set the Difficulty

In a Challenge when two opponents face each other, the Difficulty for a player character is set by the number of successes their opponent rolls. Guide characters build their pool of dice in the same way as player characters.

When it comes to other Challenges – those without an active opponent – the Guide sets a Difficulty and rolls that number of dice.

An easy task will have a Difficulty of 3. For a player character who has any relevant Traits, success is as good as automatic; at that Difficulty level, a No-roll Challenge is usually more appropriate. However, for each additional complicating factor in the situation, the Guide adds 3 to the Difficulty. A 'typical' task – routine, but with some added difficulties, and therefore worth rolling – has a Difficulty of 6. The following examples also note how many successes would be needed were they being handled as No-roll Challenges.

> **Easy Tests (Difficulty 3; two successes needed)**: Sneaking around at night when nobody is paying too much attention; Climbing a tree; Picking an ordinary lock; A performance to impress a pub full of happy drunk people.

> **Routine Tests (Difficulty 6; four successes needed)**: Climbing a crumbling wall; Finding a particular book in an uncatalogued library; Surviving a winter's night in the Apennine Mountains without suffering harm; Deactivating a trap; Sneaking past guards at night; Haggling with a merchant over a crucial and expensive item.

> **Challenging Tests (Difficulty 9; six successes needed)**: Deactivating a complex clockwork trap; Sneaking past guards at night with a small group; Climbing the outside of the Leaning Tower of Pisa.

> **Formidable Tests (Difficulty 12; eight successes needed)**: Climbing a tall crumbling wall at night with no light; Sneaking past highly alert guards by day; Climbing the outside of the Leaning Tower of Pisa immediately after a rain shower.

> **Legendary Tests (Difficulty 15; ten successes needed)**: Sneaking past highly alert guards by day when there is no cover; Deactivating a trap created by a renowned artificer when under time pressure; Climbing the outside of the Leaning Tower of Pisa during a storm after you have just been drenched in olive oil.

Create Scene Traits

During an adventure, the Guide will describe the surroundings and may choose to pick out one or two descriptions to turn into Scene Traits. A handy technique is to write them on a card and place them on the table for everyone playing to see (and perhaps use) – you may wish to use wipeable plastic cards to note Scene Traits so that they can be reused. The Guide will assign the Trait a value, typically 1d or 2d for a normal situation such as a rainstorm, 3d or 4d for pretty extreme circumstances, and 5d as the effective maximum. As a nice touch, you might want to keep a separate pool of dice with a distinctive colour for Scene Trait values so that, when the Scene Trait card is put on the table, the relevant number of dice can be placed on it. Then, when a character uses the Scene Trait in a Challenge, they can pick up the dice and include them in their pool. As the dice are a different colour, everyone will see if the Scene Trait made any difference to their success total.

Players may also suggest Scene Traits to the Guide or create them by the character's actions, and put them on the table. The Guide will adjudicate if they are acceptable and assign them a value. Of course, they can be used by the Guide characters too.

Example Scene Traits: Sharply Illuminated Street; Rough, Pockmarked Wall; A Respectful Stillness in the Air; A Sudden Fog That Envelopes Everything; It's Party Time!; Thick Undergrowth.

Build Your Pool of Dice

This is the core of Challenge resolution. Begin with the **relevant Attribute** that you are using in the Challenge. The Attribute value is the number of dice you use to start your pool. Then choose **one supporting Trait**. It should usually be one of those associated with the Attribute you are using. However, you may find that, on occasion, another one of the Attributes has a more relevant Trait to fit the description of the action. In that instance, either of the Attributes could receive Damage Traits if the Challenge fails, with the winner choosing which.

If you have any **useful equipment,** you can add one item's dice into your pool. Equipment dice can be anything. In combat they will probably be weapons, but in a social Challenge they could be impressive robes, and in an intellectual Challenge they might be books on the subject at hand.

If you choose to declare a **Goal**, add your Goal die or dice into the pool. Goals can be used only three times per game session, and a Long-term Goal only once.

If there are **Scene Traits** in play that might be used to your advantage, add the value of one of them to your dice pool as well.

One **other character** can provide you with extra dice by describing how their actions help and by using one of their Traits. If the value of the helping character's Trait is equal to or less than yours then they add one of their dice to your pool. If the value of their Trait is higher than the one you are using then they can add two of their dice instead. Make sure everyone is using different coloured dice, so you can see if any of their dice contribute to your total successes.

Opponents may have exploitable **Flaws** or carry **Damage Traits**. You may pick one, and the Guide will give you dice equal to the value of the Flaw or Damage.

Check if there are any **Scale** differences in play. Apply automatic successes as appropriate. Scale typically applies when participants are of very different sizes or speeds (p. 144).

The Guide is always at liberty to provide one or two bonus dice to the player if the description of the action is particularly moving, entertaining, or well thought out.

Optionally, if the Guide feels that the selected Trait is a stretch for the Challenge, they may add dice to the Difficulty or the active opponent's pool. Typically, this will be a number of dice up to half the value (rounded up) of the Trait that is being used by the player character.

And that's your pool of dice!

The Guide can choose to add dice to their pool, too. A Guide character may have the same options, but the Guide may also draw on Traits of the player character if appropriate, such as a Flaw or simply a Trait that actually works against the character this time round.

Example: Gianluca of Forlì has the Trait Ghibelline Through and Through 3d. Where that is known, or he chooses to reveal it, he can use that as a bonus to attempt to make alliances with fellow Ghibellines. However, the Ghibellines are loyal to the Holy Roman Empire, so when one of the Emperor's agents is trying to persuade Gianluca to smuggle a message to one of their agents in besieged Assisi, the Guide can use that Trait in support of the agent's Honeyed Words 4d.

MANAGING THE SIZE OF YOUR DICE POOL

If you want to keep the number of dice in your pool down to a manageable number then you can, at the Guide's discretion, flexibly blend average successes with dice rolled. The rule is simple. For every three whole dice you remove from your pool, give yourself two successes. Then, roll the remainder of your dice to see how many more successes you get. In this way, at your gaming table, you can always restrict dice pools to no more than a certain number of actual dice thrown.

For example, if you have a pool of thirteen dice, you may choose to remove six dice to give you four successes. Then roll the remaining seven dice to try and get some more.

Roll the Dice and See Who Wins

Now that both you and the opposition (whether another character or a Difficulty set by the Guide) have pools of dice, it's time to roll them!

- Each die showing a 6 counts as two successes.
- Each die showing a 4 or 5 counts as one success.
- Each die showing a 1, 2, or 3 counts as no successes.

The side with the greater number of successes wins and can describe what happens as framed by the desired outcomes of the Challenge. This outcome may be tempered by the Margin of Victory (p. 134).

If the result is a tie, with the same number of successes on each side, the Guide decides the most interesting outcome to move the story along. If the player is deemed the winner, the Guide will introduce a new complication to the scene.

Example: Vittorio is climbing the face of the 100m-tall St Mark's Belltower in Venice to try and prevent some crazed anarchists from letting loose a slowly deflating balloon bearing a flask of Greek Fire. He has a total of five dice in his pool. His player calls out a Scene Trait of Rough Brick Wall, which the Guide gives one die. Vittorio adds it to his pool of dice. Determined to get to the top, his player creates and declares a personal Goal (see p. 146), 'Get to the top of this damned tower!' The Guide also gives this Goal a value of one die. Altogether, Vittorio now has seven dice for his climbing attempt. The Wall has a Difficulty of 7d. The Guide decides to use six dice from the Difficulty to generate four automatic successes, and to roll one die for some variability, whereas Vittorio decides to roll all seven.

Vittorio gets 6,6,5,4,3,3,1 – six successes

The climb Difficulty gets four successes, plus a die roll of 1 – four successes

Vittorio ascends the tower without alerting anyone. Perched on the roof, he hears the anarchists start to inflate the balloon, gleefully anticipating the havoc they plan to unleash on the sleeping city. Now that he's up here, he just has to decide how to deal with them.

MULTI-ROLL CHALLENGES

Multi-roll Challenges are just the same as One-roll Challenges, except that the outcome is resolved through a number of rounds of dice throwing. You can choose to use a Multi-roll approach for any Challenge; it really just depends on how much focus you want to put on the action. It works best for an important or climactic confrontation, or a critical challenge where there is scope for a meaningful back-and-forth.

The procedure for Multi-roll Challenges is similar to the simpler One-roll Challenge:

1. Check intent and desired outcomes.
2. Set the Difficulty or assemble the opposing pool from an adversary.
3. Select, or create, and share any applicable Scene Traits.
4. Build the player character's dice pool.
5. Roll the dice, total your successes, and see who wins that round.
6. Apply the result from the Margin of Victory table.

If the winner gets a Minor Victory or better, they gain narrative control and can continue or change the nature of the next roll, creating a new Challenge description if it makes sense in the flow of the shared narrative.

Continue until one side concedes or is removed due to damage (p. 135).

DIFFERENT KINDS OF CHALLENGES

This section covers some ways in which Challenges can be structured and run to reflect different circumstances and situations.

COMBAT

Many roleplaying games have an extensive combat section that provides a more detailed set of rules to cover this exciting and dangerous aspect of play. In *Gran Meccanismo*, however, all contests are treated in the same way and there are no special rules for combat. Here are a few tips to make use of the game rules to highlight some typical factors that influence the outcome of combat scenes.

Weapons, Armour, and Shields

Don't worry about keeping track of detailed lists of weapons, armour, and other equipment of warfare. Using the standard equipment bonus Trait of 1–5d is enough to address almost all such kit. Here are some sample Equipment Traits with their values:

> *Battle-worn Spear and Ragged Leather Armour 1d*
> *Good Blade and Trusty Armour 2d*
> *Master-forged Sword and the Finest German Plate Armour 3d*

Signature, New Science, or legendary weapons may have even higher-value Traits or may benefit from the effects of Scale. Some more thoughts on equipment can be found on page 150.

Combat with Multiple Player Characters

Combat will often involve all the player characters fighting another group of adversaries. Typically, this situation would be resolved using either a One-roll Challenge or a Multi-roll Challenge.

> **One-roll:** Break down the combat into a number of separate One-roll Challenges, where each player character faces one or more opponents or offers help to an engaged ally. Each player resolves the Challenge covering the combat between their character and opposition. Each character may have different outcomes – some will win and some will lose. The Guide interprets the overall outcome of the combat scene based on the individual results of each player character.

Multi-roll: As with the One-roll variant, except now each roll is a round of action. The Margin of Victory, and resulting Damage Traits, are applied to each individual combatant as they happen. Rounds continue until one side gives up or loses.

Alternatively, have each side pick a leader. The leader then assembles their dice pool in the usual way whilst all the other protagonists describe their actions and contribute further dice to the leader's pool. With each leader's full pool collected, the dice are rolled and the collective outcome decided. The Guide then adjudicates the outcome and parcels out Damage Traits, with the lion's share usually going to the losing side. The winning side gets the outcome that they wanted.

Combat Scene Traits

Much of the dynamic detail in combat scenes can be modelled by using Scene Traits, writing down the description and assigning a value in the usual way. Often the Scene Trait will be particularly useful to one or other of the sides in the combat and will suggest particular tactics. Below are a few examples:

Surprise Ambush 3d: One side can use this Scene Trait for either a One-roll Challenge or the first round of a Multi-roll Challenge.

Holding the High Ground 4d: One side can use this Scene Trait for as long as it applies in the narrative.

Outnumbered! 1–4d: Add a bonus die to the opponent's dice pool for every extra opponent after the first, up to five opponents against a single player character.

Poor Footing 1d: Both sides can use this Scene Trait for a bonus die, unless their opponent has the poise to fight on uneven ground unperturbed.

DEBATES, SEDUCTIONS, AND PERSUASIONS

Human interactions can often be as complex and conflicted as combat skirmishes. In *Gran Meccanismo*, the same principles apply but the details change. 'Weapons' may be anything from especially fine clothes to impress a banker whom you want to finance your latest venture, to an extravagant gift to soften a beloved's heart, or a vial of the blood of St Januarius brandished at a key moment in your speech to the Papal Curia. Special items should have their own Trait value, and Wealth (p. 148) can sometimes be used to procure what you may need.

Likewise, Scene Traits are every bit as important, depending on the nature of the Challenge: *Low Light and Soft Music* 2d is likely going to be relevant for a seduction, but probably somewhat less so for a theological debate.

EXPLORATORY CHALLENGES

Sometimes, a player will want to achieve something relatively broad, whilst not really having a specific outcome in mind. For example, Sister Paola, the nun-turned-Vatican-spycatcher, is trying to find out whether or not there really is a ring of French conspirators in the Swiss Guard. Whilst, in theory this could be played out as a whole session unto itself, it would require Sister Paola's player and the Guide to get into the fine details of the investigation and there probably wouldn't be much for the other players to do in the meantime – plus it's not all that important to the focus of the current adventure. As such, it's decided that it would be far better to resolve it quickly. This could be done with a regular One-roll Challenge, but that lends itself to a simple success or failure result, which can be a little bland. Instead, to make things more interesting, the Guide secretly sets a number of successes that will reveal the whole story and calls for Sister Paola to assemble her pool and throw the dice. If Sister Paola fails to achieve the full number of successes, the Guide will nonetheless pass on snippets of information reflecting how close she got, but without letting the player know just how complete a picture this may be. A similar approach can be used for other open-ended activities that are best resolved quickly, such as Clocking (p. 156).

LONG-TERM CHALLENGES

Challenges can take any length of time. Indeed, a whole year's worth of trading, studying, or leading a mercenary company could be resolved in a single roll. However, sometimes a Challenge is best approached episodically, happening behind or between the main action. Examples include a French invasion of Italy taking place whilst the heroes live their day-to-day lives, or one character's literary duel with her rival, fought out pamphlet by pamphlet. This type of Challenge can be resolved by separate, individual One-roll Challenges as and when, but can also be treated as an episodic Multi-roll Challenge, especially if the player characters' actions or other factors may influence each round. To take this approach, simply make a note of the respective dice pools and the current state of play, then roll the next round at the beginning or end of each gaming session, or whenever seems most appropriate. This is an excellent way to give a sense of major events happening in the world, and for the players to affect it. See page 161 for more on this concept.

> **Example:** *War! Milan's armies are marching on the Venetian Terraferma – the Serene Republic's mainland territories. The Guide could simply dictate what happens, as the player characters are not directly involved, but as one character comes from Venice and another has trading interests in the Terraferma, they feel it is worth turning into an episodic Challenge. They decide that Milan's forces, which have been preparing all spring, have 10d and Venice's unprepared defences have 7d, rising by 2d each round that they survive. The first attack sees Milan winning by two successes, for a Solid Victory (see Outcomes (p. 134), so Venice suffers a penalty, Demoralised People 2d.*

In the next session, the Guide rolls again; it's now Milan's 10d against Venice's 7d (7d, +2d reinforcement, -2d penalty). The dice are kinder to Venice this time, but the Milanese still take a Slight Victory and Venice suffers Disagreements amongst Generals 1d, although, as noted above, typically only the higher Damage Trait applies, so this has no immediate impact beyond nudging the cumulative impact closer to the 7 it will need for Venice's forces to be broken. They cannot expect the same luck twice and, at this point, the players decide that they'd rather not see the France-backed Milanese extend their power. As such, they decide to spend a session politicking with the bandits of Trento (with whom one of them has connections) to encourage them to raid the over-extended Milanese supply lines. In the next session, the Milanese suffer a one-off 3d penalty as a result, so it is Milan's 7d (10d, -3d penalty) versus Venice's 7d (7d, +2d reinforcements, -2d penalty), giving La Serenissima more of a chance to finally turn the tables.

MOOKS

Low-grade nameless adversaries often appear to overwhelm heroes, compensating for their lack of narrative presence by force of numbers and misplaced optimism. They will typically have low Attribute and Trait values, or more likely, a single fairly low Trait, such as *Brutish Thug* 4d.

Mooks can simply be abstracted into a single antagonist, such as *Bunch of Thugs* 8d or the like, and dealt with in a One-roll Challenge, or they can be grouped into gangs of about five mooks. In this scenario, one thug acts as the leader and assembles their dice pool in the usual way, whilst the other four are represented using the *Outnumbered* 1–4d Scene Trait (p. 126). So, if one hero is facing five *Brutish Thug* 4d opponents, they will get four dice for the leader and a total of +4d for the rest, giving a substantial eight dice overall, with all mooks sharing the outcome of the roll. If the Margins of Victory table is being used then every 1d Damage Trait instead removes one mook from the fight, which will lower the number of dice they can roll if they get another chance in a Multi-roll Challenge.

This is more immediately relevant in a physical fight, but it can be used for a variety of many-against-one contests, such as a debate against a hostile panel of scholars or an attempt to bring order to an especially unruly class of students.

OUTCOMES

The outcome of a Challenge can often be narrated by the Guide based on the desired outcome determined at the start of the Challenge, with the side that rolls the most successes getting the outcome they want. For a more granular approach, especially in the round-by-round contests of Multi-roll Challenges, the Margin of Victory determines the extent of the victory and the consequential damage – the greater the difference between the success totals, the greater the consequences.

MARGIN OF VICTORY

The Margin of Victory table is used to determine the consequences of defeat. The amount you win by is the value of the Damage Trait applied to the loser. When using the Margin of Victory table, player characters win ties narrowly in that they inflict a +1 Difficulty on their opponent for the next round, which means the relevant player character will add one bonus die into their own pool.

	MARGIN OF VICTORY	
Margin	Victory Level	Damage to the Loser
0	Knife Edge	Scratch: Next roll at +1d Difficulty
1	Slight	Hurt: Damage Trait 1d
2	Solid	Wound: Damage Trait 2d
3	Major	Trauma: Damage Trait 3d
4	Emphatic	Incapacitated: Damage Trait 4d and removed from Challenge.
5+	Complete	Enough to permanently remove character from play.

Damage applies only when losing a Challenge that has personal consequences, such as injury, mental trauma, or personal humiliation. This is not appropriate in every situation. Even when damage is appropriate for a failed outcome, the Guide may wish to cap the damage to a 1d Trait – it's very rare for someone literally to die of embarrassment.

Damage Traits

A Damage Trait is a new negative Trait that is applied to the Body, Mind, or Soul Attribute – generally the one that was used in the challenge, but the Guide may occasionally rule otherwise. This Damage Trait can be used by the opposition in their hand of dice if the Attribute is in play for a particular Challenge.

A character can have multiple Damage Traits applied to one or more of their Attributes, depending on the nature of the damage. The highest-value Damage Trait relevant to that Challenge is applied as a bonus to your opponent in any Challenges for as long as it persists, including the next round in a Multi-roll Challenge. Usually, that means a Damage Trait on the Attribute in use, but circumstances may dictate otherwise. For example, Genoese pirate Pietro has the Body Damage Trait *Gash to the Face* 1d and the Soul Damage Trait *Sudden Loss of Confidence* 3d. If he is challenged to a fight, the Guide may rule that the latter ought to be applied, even if it is a Body-based Challenge.

If the total of all Damage Trait values within a particular Attribute is greater than the Attribute value itself, the character is knocked out of play, which could mean that they're knocked unconscious, they flee the scene, they're laughed out of court, or whatever is most appropriate. Once the damage has healed enough, such that the values are equal to or less than the Attribute value, the character can return to play. Optionally, the Guide may allow the character to continue in play, but without being able to use the Attribute or associated Traits until they have healed.

OPTIONAL RULE: RESILIENT HEROES

If you wish to play more resilient heroes, have them able to withstand total Damage Trait values up to twice the affected Attribute. So, if a character has a Body Trait of 3, they would be able to continue in play with physical Damage Traits up to a combined value of 6 (for example, Hurt 1d, Wound 2d, and Trauma 3d) rather than 4. However, remember that only the Trait with the highest value counts as a bonus to your opponent's pool or the task Difficulty.

NPCs expressed as a single core Trait who suffer Damage Traits are knocked out of a Challenge when they reach a set Damage value determined by the Guide. Typically, for your average NPC, this will be set at either 2 or 3. For more impressive single-Trait NPCs, this can increase to 4 or 5.

An Emphatic Victory, dealing a Damage Trait of 4d to the character, is incapacitating – the character is knocked out of the current Challenge, even if they have a score of 4 or more for that Attribute. This reflects a severe attack that is more than can be borne in one blow. The advantage in having Attributes of 4 or higher is that they can soak up lesser Damage Traits for longer, keeping the character in the action.

A Complete Victory permanently knocks the character out of the shared story. This will be negotiated between the Guide and the player; see Cliffhangers and Lucky Escapes (p. 186).

Some example Damage Traits follow, grouped by severity and attribute.

Scratch: This is a relatively minor setback – not even a full Damage Trait, really. It isn't generally necessary to write down Scratch-level damage because it only lasts until the next roll or for a period of in-game time determined by the Guide. Here are some example Scratch Traits:

Body: *'Tis But a Scratch, Pulled Muscle, Bruised, Winded*

Mind: *Distracted, Disturbed Thoughts, On the Tip of My Tongue, Strange Dream*

Soul: *Slightly Embarrassed, Cross, Taken Aback*

Hurt: This is serious damage that impairs the performance of the character. Each Hurt Trait has a value of 1d, which is added to any Difficulty or opponent's pool of dice where the character is using that Attribute in a Challenge. Some example Hurt Traits include:

Body: *Bad Gash, Sprained Ankle, Weeping Sores*

Mind: *Confused, Flustered, Can't Remember, Dazed*

Soul: *Saddened, Angry, Embarrassed, Nervous*

Wound and trauma: These represent more serious damage, and potentially more lasting impairments, rated at 2d or 3d, respectively. Here are some examples:

Body: *Gaping Wound, Torn Muscle, Smashed Ankle, Broken Rib, Concussion*

Mind: *Unhinged, Lost and Confused, Mind's a Total Blank*

Soul: *Depressed, Crisis of Confidence, Bad Reputation, Outright Terrified*

Incapacitated or worse: When incapacitated, the character is immediately knocked out of the current Challenge. They have been seriously damaged and will take some time to recover. This applies even if the damaged character has an Attribute of 4 or more. If the opponent's Margin of Victory is greater than 4, it could be that the character has been permanently removed from the game – this tends to happen in combat and other dangerous situations, but it can also happen if the character has lost a loved one or witnessed great horrors. Each of these Traits is rated at 4d, some examples being:

Body: Unconscious, Smashed Ribs, Terrible Scarring

Mind: Gibbering Wreck, Unconscious, Crippling Self-doubt, Amnesia

Soul: Suicidal, Overwhelming Rage, Banished and Reviled, Panicked, Besotted, Seriously Questioning Life Choices

Damage Traits do not generally 'stack' – if a character receives two 1d Body Damage Traits then all Challenges using the Body Attribute would still only have +1d Difficulty, unless the Guide decides otherwise in exceptional circumstances.

Example: Bruno has been charged with using forged letters of credit – a very serious charge – as part of a hostile take-over by his rival, the perfidious Roman exile Don Pasquale. Bruno is arguing his case in court, which the Guide has chosen to run as a Multi-roll Challenge. Through good luck and good argument, Bruno wins the first round by three, translating to a Major Victory and a Trauma Damage Trait. Pasquale's lawyer suffers the Damage Trait Caught Out in a Lie 3d. However, this is an expensive and experienced professional, with the Trait Subtle Litigator 6d, so the Guide rules that he is still in the contest (his dice pool is more than six, incidentally, thanks to the support of a suborned witness and impressive, if forged, evidence). In the next round, Bruno gains an extra 3d due to his opponent's blunder. He moves in for the kill, invoking his Goal 'Protect my reputation' for an extra die, giving him a total of +4d for his next roll. He wins two more successes than the lawyer for a Solid Victory and a further Damage Trait: Undermined Argument 2d. This makes a total of 5d worth of Damage Traits to the lawyer, bringing the total damage to almost equal with his Trait. He is still in the fight, but Bruno still gets a +3d (remember, only the highest Damage Trait applies). If the lawyer takes another 1d or more damage, he will be knocked out of the contest, which in this instance means he'll be forced to close the case and withdraw Don Pasquale's accusations.

Powering Through

For some Challenges, a player character may be determined to succeed, no matter what the cost. In this case, use the usual rules for Challenges but, if the character loses the roll, they Power Through and succeed, suffering damage according to the degree of failure in the process, increased by one level on the Margin of Victory table (this does mean that it would be possible for both sides in the contest to be killed). The Guide should make this clear when they set up the Challenge, and it is always at the Guide's discretion. It certainly should not be the norm, but can be reserved for special occasions where the story demands a dramatic resolution.

Example: *Bruno has had enough of Don Pasquale and launches a concerted attack on his rival's reputation, with the explicit goal of forcing him out of Florence once and for all. With the Guide's approval, he says that he will accomplish this, whatever the cost. This will be a social contest, based on Soul. Mustering his resources and calling in his favours, Bruno has ten dice. Don Pasquale has just seven dice, but as he is an aristocrat fighting in the social realm, the Guide decides he has Scale 1 (p. 144), providing two automatic successes. Bruno rolls six successes whilst Pasquale rolls five, which, with his Scale advantage, gives him a total of seven successes. It's a nasty battle of politics and slander. Technically, Pasquale has won, but as this is a Powering Through Challenge, Pasquale does indeed decamp to try his luck in Bologna. However, Bruno has suffered a Slight Defeat, which would normally mean he is Hurt, but, because Powering Through increases the effect on the Margin of Victory table by one level, in this case he takes a Wound. The Guide decides that some of the mud sticks, and Bruno now has the Soul Damage Trait Could the Rumours Be True? 2d.*

Massimo is a typical bravo, a back-streets thug from Lucca putting on the airs of high birth. He still kills for money, though.

HEALING

Damage traits typically heal over time, whether in a session or in between sessions. Choose whichever is shortest from the following table and, after that amount of time, a Damage Trait goes away. Damage Traits applied to different Attributes can, under appropriate circumstances, heal at the same time (so that a character resting for an in-game week in the supportive company of their family could heal a 1d Body and a 1d Soul Damage Trait together). Generally, Damage Traits applied to the same Attribute heal one at a time, in ascending order of magnitude. So a character with two 1d and one 3d Damage Traits on the same Attribute would heal one 1d first (generally, the player chooses which), then another 1d, then the 3d Damage Trait: something that would take five sessions of play, or three months and two weeks of in-game time.

HEALING		
Damage Trait	Natural Recovery	Healing Difficulty
Hurt: Damage Trait 1d	End of session, or one week of in-game time	3d
Wound: Damage Trait 2d	Two sessions, or one month of in-game time	6d
Trauma: Damage Trait 3d	Three sessions, or three months of in-game time	9d
Incapacitated: Damage Trait 4d	Four sessions, or four months of in-game time	12d
Complete: Character removed from play	Guide determines the time, if recovery is even possible	15d

A Healing Challenge is allowed for each Damage Trait if the character receives suitable treatment to repair the damage, which could be anything from seeing a doctor to treat a wound to a night out on the town to restore good spirits, depending on the nature of the impairment. The Guide can rule otherwise, but typically only one attempt to heal each Attribute can be made in each session of play. If successful against the Difficulty noted in the table, it reduces the Damage Trait by a number of levels as determined by the Margin of Victory. So, a Major Victory, scoring three successes higher than the Healing Difficulty, would heal 3d worth of Attribute damage. If there is any remaining damage, the value that is left must heal naturally as per the Natural Recovery column.

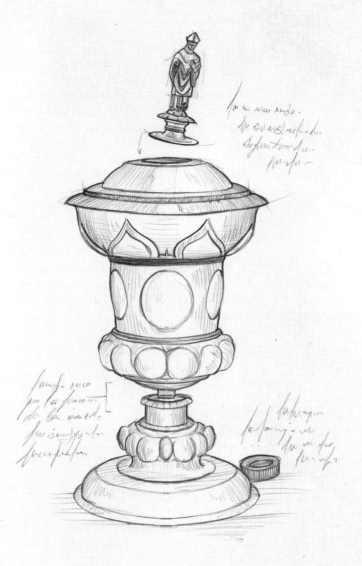

The filtration goblet is a famous alchemical device — note the Statuette of Albertus Magnus, patron saint of the sciences — in which a variety of filters can be fitted into the lid, each of which has its own special use, from filtering poisons and toxic mixtures from water to denaturing the alcohol from wine, simply by pouring a liquid in through the top. It is rumoured that there are even filters that will turn a wholesome drink of perfectly normal wine into illicit drugs and poisons.

Filter Liquid +3d.

NUDGES

Nudges give players an extra edge to influence the outcome of Challenges in their character's favour. Starting characters have 3 Nudges, and thereafter they start each game session with a number of Nudges equal to their highest Trait. After the dice are rolled, each Nudge allows a player to shift the outcome of a single die by one step. So, a die that has landed as a failure (1–3) can be upgraded to a success and a die that is a success (4–5) can be upgraded to a double success (6). A double success can't be affected by a Nudge.

The Guide starts a session with two Nudges for each player, and can use them to boost the results of antagonists or environmental challenges.

Nudges are made available at the start of a game session and they can only be spent by the owning character. Nudges apply to your pool of dice once rolled – a single die can be Nudged multiple times (from a failure to a double success). Effectively, Nudges provide a pool of extra successes if you really need to win a Challenge, limited by the number of dice in your pool.

Nudges can also be spent to temporarily increase a Trait that is being used to help another character by 1d per Nudge. This may increase the value of the helping Trait above the one being helped, thus allowing the helper to give two dice instead of one.

You can use as many Nudges as you wish on an individual dice roll. However, they are a finite resource, so spend them wisely (or recklessly, if that's your style), according to your character and the situation.

Nudges are refreshed at the start of the next game session. A refresh gives the character a number of Nudges equal to their highest Trait value, unless they already have more Nudges, in which case they simply keep those they already have. If a game session is very long, or it has involved a large number of rolled Challenges, the Guide can choose to refresh the Nudges at any time. This will also refresh Guide Nudges.

Guides can also distribute Nudges during a session to reward a player for the things that are important to the group at the table – be that good roleplay, cunning plans, impassioned speeches, allowing others into the spotlight, cooperative play, or anything else that the Guide wants to see from the players.

FLAWS

Some Traits will generally count against a character. These are called Flaws. Flaw Traits can entail greed, laziness, cowardice, obsessions, dangerous vices, and personal enemies, amongst other things. Many of the best Traits are written in such a way that they can be either a boon or a bane depending on the circumstance, but only those which are primarily negative count as Flaws.

At the start of a game session, a player can suggest to the Guide that a Trait counts as a Flaw for that session. During play, the Guide may then bring forth a situation or suggest a course of action associated with this Flaw. If you agree to it, life may get complicated for your character, as the Guide will use the Flaw in a Challenge against you. As a reward for playing along, you get an extra Nudge straight away and an extra Minor Advancement (p. 158) at the end of the session.

You can also suggest a course of action inspired by a Flaw during a session, intended to make things harder for your character. If the Guide agrees, you get an extra Minor Advancement at the end of the game session. You can only gain two Minor Advancements in this way per game session: one for a course of action suggested by you, and one for a course of action suggested by the guide.

SCALE

Some things are on a greater than normal human scale. No hero, however experienced, is going to be able to wrestle an elephant, flip a Florentine turtle-tank, perform complicated mental arithmetic quicker than the Gran Meccanismo, or kick through the walls of the Sforza Castle. In these circumstances, the Guide may simply rule that it is impossible or, if the player really wants to try or has a cunning plan in mind, let a contest go ahead with a Scale advantage.

Likewise, sometimes characters have in-built advantages. In most social situations, an aristocrat is going to be treated differently, and any attempt to debate theology with the Pope is going to be an uphill battle. Particularly extraordinary items, such as the most exclusive inventions of the New Science, the finest creations of artists such as Michelangelo, and the most sacred relics, may also have a Scale advantage in appropriate circumstances.

In such cases, the Guide will apply a Scale advantage quantified by a number of automatic successes added to the outcome of relevant Challenges. For human distinctions, this will typically be from 1 to 4. A commoner trying to out-condescend an aristocrat might face an opponent with a +2 success Scale advantage, for example, whilst the Pope could count on a +4 success Scale bonus in that disagreement over scripture. Of course, this only applies in the context where the Scale difference is relevant – there's no Scale advantage involved if the commoner is arm-wrestling the nobleman or if the Pope is involved in a drinking contest!

In other cases, the Scale advantage can be +6, or even higher! The Sforza Castle, for example, has the Trait *High, Strong Walls* 8d. If someone wants to climb them, that's a Difficulty 8 Challenge. If someone wants to smash them with their bare hands, a +8 success Scale advantage might also be appropriate.

Luisa Fontana, the elegant courtesan from Milan, doesn't let her disdain for the Sicilians' provincial ways show, as she hopes to bag the Spanish general Angel Maria Puebla before he is recalled to Madrid after his tour commanding the garrison at Palermo.

GOALS

Goals represent the short- and long-term objectives your player character is focused on. You may invoke your Goals up to three times per game session, when one of them is relevant in a Challenge. Major, Long-term Goals, rated at 5d, can be invoked only once in a game session. You don't have to use three different Goals; you can invoke the same Moderate, Mid-term (3d) or Minor, Short-term (1d) Goal up to three times if you want.

- If you declare a Goal before you roll the dice, you get bonus dice equal to the value of the Goal. The bonus can be used for only one roll.
- If you declare a Mid- or Long-term Goal *after* you roll the dice, you can do *one* of the following:
  - Reroll all of your dice.
  - Improve your Victory Level by one on the Margin of Victory in the table (if you are successful).
  - Turn a defeat into a tie. Just as for any other failure when invoking a Goal, this will cost you some Doubt, as described below.

If you achieve a Mid- or Long-term Goal in a game session, you get an extra Minor Advancement or Significant Advancement respectively, at the end of the game session. Additionally, you can replace the Goal with another Goal without paying the cost of a Minor Advancement.

Example: Sister Paola has the Mid-term Goal 'Identify the French spymaster in Rome' 3d. During the course of her hunt, she realises she will have to try and leap from one roof to another. This is not exactly the 50-year-old investigator's thing, and she can only muster Body 2 and, with the Guide's approval, the Mind Trait Think of a Way around the Problem 3d with a penalty of -1d, as she applies her wits to considering trajectories. Even with the Scene Trait of Close-packed Buildings 1d, she only has 5d (2+3-1+1), against a Difficulty 8 Challenge, and she's all out of Nudges.

She could invoke her Goal before the roll to give herself three extra dice. Or she could wait until she sees if the dice are kind. She opts for the latter. Predictably, she fails, and badly: as the dice stand, would take a Solid (-3d) defeat. Rather than try again, she invokes her Goal to turn her defeat into a tie, at the cost of acquiring a Doubt. As the Guide gets to adjudicate ties, they decide Sister Paola makes it to the roof but her foot loudly smashes through a tile, getting stuck, whilst voices raised in anger can be heard from the room below.

DOUBTS

If, you invoke a Mid- or Long-term Goal and lose the roll, you gain a Doubt Trait. You also gain a Doubt when you use a Goal to turn a failure in a Challenge into a tie. This new Trait is associated with the Goal, in the same way that Damage Traits are associated with an Attribute. The initial value of a Doubt Trait is the level of damage inflicted when you failed the challenge (or the damage that would have been inflicted, if you used the Goal to turn a defeat into a tie).

The following rules apply to Doubt Traits:

- The dice from the Doubt Trait are always used as a bonus to the opposition when you invoke that Goal.
- If a Goal has an associated Doubt Trait, you can invoke the Goal only *before* you roll.
- If you succeed in a Challenge when using a Goal with an associated Doubt Trait, reduce the value of the Doubt Trait by 1.
- If you fail in a Challenge when using a Goal with an associated Doubt Trait, increase the value of the Doubt by 1 instead of adding a new Doubt.
- If the Doubt Trait reaches a level equal to or higher than the Goal, both the Goal and Doubt are removed. You will have to use a Minor Advancement (p. 158) to acquire a new one.
- If you achieve a Goal with an associated Doubt Trait, remove it along with the Goal.

Example: *Sister Paola would have taken a Damage Trait at 3d had she not invoked her Goal, so she now acquires a Doubt Trait of that value, which is enough to remove the Goal. If, though, it had been her Long-term Goal, with a value of 5d, then the Goal would have acquired a Doubt, such as I'm Just Not up to This 3d. Then, whenever she invoked her 5d Goal in the future, her opponent would get a bonus of 3d.*

WEALTH AND EQUIPMENT

Even though player characters may be merchants and traders, or simply greedy, this is not a game in which every florin and flask of oil ought to be tallied and tracked. Instead, for the flow of play, Wealth is treated as a Trait and most equipment is simply abstracted into bonus dice. Characters are given a Wealth level when first created, typically derived from their profession. What's really important is how this Wealth, or lack of it, can be used to propel ideas for stories in the game.

WEALTH

In many of the stories that will be played out at your gaming table, characters will have plenty of opportunities to gain Wealth through fair means and foul. Discovered treasure, promotion to a position of power, unexpected inheritance – anything could happen. As the Wealth system is a convenient abstraction, the rules for acquiring Wealth are also suitably easy to apply.

Gaining and Losing Wealth

During a game session, characters may pick up extra funds, whether by looting a sack of ducats or being paid for some task or other. However, this is generally considered part of the regular ebb and flow of funds and will not affect their basic Wealth level.

Rather, if in-game circumstances would seem to allow it – such as if the character is promoted to a higher position or comes across some great treasure – then a Significant Advancement can be used to cement this and increase their Wealth by 1 (to up to 5d). It takes a Major Advancement to raise Wealth further, to 6d or 7d (see p. 159).

Likewise, ordinary expenses commensurate to a character's Wealth will not lower it – for a Wealth 2d commoner, this means staying in cheap accommodations and owning the tools of their trade, whilst for a Wealth 4d merchant this could include throwing an extravagant party and occasionally hiring a bodyguard. The important thing is for this not to be abused – the Guide may impose a temporary or permanent penalty on Wealth for excesses, whether because the player is trying to game the system or simply because the character is living beyond their means.

Using Wealth

If the Cost (p. 151) of a desired item or service is less than or equal to the character's Wealth, they can acquire the resource as and when, unless the Guide decides that it is not currently available. Clearly, this could be open to abuse if a player just wants to acquire lots of things for their character, so 'overspending' will result in the reduction of Wealth levels (permanently or temporarily) or the creation of Debt, as determined by the Guide.

Characters can only attempt to get items with a Cost 1 greater than their Wealth. Any more is simply beyond their buying power, though there are other options, such as pooling wealth and taking out loans. This requires a Wealth Challenge against the Cost, resolved as a One-roll Challenge. At the Guide's discretion, other Traits can be used as bonuses, such as *Skilful Haggling* or a social relationship to a potential seller, but this should be handled with caution, as it can lead to strange results. The Difficulty can also be increased by conditions (such as scarcity or sudden demand) and the seller, who may also be a skilful haggler or simply *Greedy* 4d.

If the character wins, they get the item without damaging their Wealth rating. If not, they can either choose not to get whatever they were after or choose to get it, but with their Wealth taking damage according to the Margin of Victory, in the form of Debt. This could knock out their Wealth entirely if they overstretch their resources.

A character can choose to Power Through and accept Debt, though again within reason – no pauper is going to be able to borrow enough to buy himself a castle! The best rule of thumb is that the maximum such extension is equal to half the character's Wealth.

Pooling Funds

Characters can pool their Wealth together to purchase an item; however, this signifies that they are stretching their resources to acquire whatever it is that they're after. Their combined Wealth level is equal to the highest Wealth amongst the characters pooling funds, plus 1 per additional character, up to a maximum of +2d. Upon acquiring the item, everyone involved temporarily has their Wealth reduced by 1, which will take either in-game activity or a Minor Advancement to restore. If, by pooling Wealth, the characters are also trying to get an item with a Cost 1 greater than their pooled Wealth, then they also must undertake a Challenge and suffer whatever consequences that may involve, in addition to the temporary Wealth reduction.

> **Example:** *Bruno has Wealth 5d and his sister Isabella has Wealth 3d. He has his eyes set on a fine, marbled mansion close to Florence's Piazza della Signoria, an acquisition that would really demonstrate his status. The Cost is 6d. They pool their resources for a pooled Wealth of 6d (5+1) and get the mansion. Bruno now has an effective Wealth 4d and Isabella an effective Wealth 2d (not that this is such a problem, as it is really just her dowry – in practice, her brother looks after her), until Bruno spends a Minor Advancement. Actually running the mansion would require Wealth 6d too, so although they get the building, they can't really afford to keep it with the host of servants it requires or maintain the building and contents over the long term. Time for Bruno to work another scheme.*

Debt

If a character suffers a serious failure when using their Wealth in a Challenge then they may acquire Debt as their Damage. Characters may also acquire Debt during play. Debt is a Trait attached to Wealth, similar to the way regular injuries apply to one of the character's Attributes and acting as a bonus for any antagonist. The Guide may also choose to apply Debt to social and similar Challenges where appropriate.

Over time, the Debt level will act as an increase to the Difficulty of acquiring equipment and living at the character's Wealth level. Debts need to be recovered and often have strings attached to them. However, focus on this only if it makes for an interesting story and drives forward the narrative in the game that you are playing.

EQUIPMENT

Generally speaking, characters are assumed to have the tools of their trade and the kind of accoutrements appropriate to their rank and their Wealth – unless they are in circumstances that dictate otherwise, whether they've been stripped naked and bound in a cellar or are traveling incognito as penniless beggars rather than wealthy noblemen. Essentially, apply common sense and consider the dramatic needs of the moment, with the Guide being the final arbiter.

Typically, the appropriate tools for a task, whether they are weapons for a fight or an artisan's tools for some crafting, will provide 1d or 2d in a Challenge. More finely crafted weapons and armour (especially rich robes) or access to a large library might give higher bonuses when in combat, impressing money lenders, or conducting research, respectively.

Generally, equipment is treated simply as a Trait bonus, some examples being: *Humungous Greatsword* (+3d), *Especially Tatty Armour* (+1d), or *Family Archive* (+3d). Particularly special equipment may have multiple bonuses.

> **Example of Special Equipment:** *The Oculars of Mars are distinctive and bulbous New Science goggles made of glass and copper that automatically focus on and zoom in to targets with a click and a whirr. They shield the wearer from extremes of light and even help provide some greater visual acuity in twilight and gloom. Blink Away Dazzle (+2d), See in the Gloom (+2d), Target Lock (+2d).*

Sometimes, a legendary item of equipment will have Traits as if it were a more noteworthy supporting character, and in particular cases it will even have a Scale advantage. Such Equipment Traits can be used as if they were a character's, provide an equipment bonus equal to the successes result in the No-roll Challenge table (p. 188), or sometimes even be the 'actor' in a Challenge, with the character effectively being its supporter. The Scale benefit will transfer across, when appropriate. See Using Constructs in a Challenge on page 155 for more on this.

Example of Legendary Equipment: Ambrosio has one of the wonderfully decorated metal vials currently stored in the Basilica di Sant'Andrea in Mantua, containing the Most Precious Blood of Christ, taken when He was on the Cross. It has the Traits Extraordinarily Decorated Vessel 6d and Holiest of Holies 5d, and Scale 1 in religious contexts. When trying to win over his new congregation – a conservative village in the deep south of the Kingdom of Naples, no place for a free-thinking Florentine city boy – he could use its Holiest of Holies 5d as the Trait to support his Soul 4d, or else his Soul 4d and Strong Conviction 3d with the artefact acting as his equipment for another three dice (the No-roll Challenge table shows that five dice give 3.3 successes, which rounds down to +3d). The first option gives him 9d (4+5), the second 10d (4+3+3), plus, in both cases, he gets one automatic success from the item's Scale bonus.

Equipment Costs

The following list gives a sense of a character's lifestyle at each Wealth level (in other words, what can be supported without undue financial stress) and the cost of specific items and services, which should be modified to reflect local circumstances and common sense.

WHAT DOES IT COST?

Cost	Lifestyle	Specific Purchases
1d	Scarcely adequate diet, basic hand-me-down clothes, live in a hovel	A pig, getting a scribe to write a letter and have it sent to the next city
2d	Live on basic food, wear cheap clothes, live in simple accommodation	Basic weapons, a mule or an old or run-down horse, a hired thug to give some commoner a kicking once, a night of distracting pleasures, a rowboat
3d	Live in a home that could accommodate a family and maybe a shop or workshop, used to eating a variety of foods, wear reasonable clothes, may have a servant	Well-made weapons and armour, a horse, a block of fine Carrara marble, holding a sumptuous meal for a respected guest
4d	Used to eating good food, wear high-status clothes, live in spacious accommodation, may have a bodyguard or skilled manservant	A war horse, a pedal-horse, hiring an assassin to kill a high-status target, holding a party that will be the talk of the city for the season, sponsoring a student through university
5d	A wealthy lifestyle, used to eating rich delicacies, wear high fashion, live in a well-appointed townhouse, have a serving staff	A Florentine spring-horse, a glider, travelling in luxury across Italy, hiring a relatively well-known artist
6d	Live in a mansion with extensive serving staff	Exquisitely made German full plate armour, building a chapel, running a vaporetto
7d	Live in a small keep	Hiring a mercenary company for a campaign, hiring a whole galley for a long journey
8d	Maintain a mercenary company	A screwcopter, a turtle-tank, building a cathedral

MAGIC AND THE NEW SCIENCE

The world of *Gran Meccanismo* is presumed to be one in which there is no magic in the usual sense of spells and incantations – instead it has the wholly fantastical devices created by the New Science. Guides may decide that religious faith has an almost magical capacity in certain specific ways, as discussed below, or choose to add magic in other ways. This is, after all, now your game. However, the working assumption here is that only the New Science, founded in Florence and just beginning to spread further, can generate extraordinary effects.

BASIC PRINCIPLES

The New Science is, of course, wholly beyond the capabilities of the time or, indeed, plausible physics. Don't worry about it. Accept that this is a world in which ornithopters can fly powered just by human muscle, that a wind-up knight can fight a human foe, and that hydraulics, clockwork, and ingenuity can create computers and possibly even full artificial intelligence.

More than anything else, the New Science is there to drive the story. It is behind the big story – the clockpunk industrial revolution taking place in Florence – sharpening political tensions across Italy and potentially triggering parallel social and religious revolutions. It can also drive individual stories, such as providing the McGuffin to drive a quest ('The Venetian agent has stolen the prototype, and your job is to get it back!'). Of course, not every character will use the New Science much or even most of the time, especially if they are not Florentine. It may be the Satanic new movement that they fear and despise, or the exciting new development they so desperately want to see, or simply something they don't think is for the likes of them. But, no matter their standing or background, they *will* know about it.

Given that, in theory, almost anything could be invented – from today's technology to cyberpunk innovations, rendered in bone, bronze, marble, or glass – the question is often how to stop the inventions from dominating the game. Here are some pointers:

One-off and Bespoke

Florence is beginning to experiment with production lines and even simple automated construction, and when it's on a full wartime footing, Venice's famous Arsenale, with its 15,000 artisans and craftspeople, can turn out one ship in a day and a half, as long as their stock of pre-made, standardised parts holds out. However, beyond certain items, like pedal-horse bicycles and the Signoria's Guard's braccie lunghe halberd-muskets, pretty much every New Science invention and gizmo made is a finely decorated one-off – time-consuming to make, expensive to buy, harder to replace.

The rumours are true! Florentine agents look down in
horror at how far advanced the French supergun is.

Breakable and Temperamental

Your fancy new three-shot revolver may be impressive, but it may jam in a way your opponent's knife will not. New Science often requires special preparations (winding the clockwork, adding fuel, or the like) and careful carriage and storage (glass vials can break, copper wires get detached). The Guide may well decide in response to a failure in a Challenge or similar situation that an item has broken, either needing repair or being rendered a useless hunk of brass and springs.

It's All about the Numbers

Here is the real secret that stops the New Science from totally destabilising the game – the Trait system means that everything is about the numbers. A *Telescoping Clockwork Sword* (+3d) may sound a lot cooler than a *Well-sharpened Sword* (+3d), and could perhaps be pressed into more unusual purposes, but in a fight they are both worth three dice, even if the former gets to be narrated in a more fun way.

MECHANISMS

There are simple artefacts of the New Science, such as pedal-horses, spring-horses (bicycles augmented with coiled springs for extra power for a short period), and multi-shot crossbows, that can be treated simply as normal equipment supporting a character's Traits, with a single rating, such as *Mechanical Abacus* (+3d).

Then there are more unusual items, which have a Trait that can actively be used. For example:

> **Mordechai's Ring:** *A distinctive ring owned and invented by the clocker Mordechai d'Israele. It is rather more than just fine jewellery. It is a wind-up watch with an alarm that silently vibrates on the finger. Plugging it into a keyhole, the user can use a Clocking Trait to pick the lock. After five minutes' winding, the tempered steel cogwheel at its heart can even grind through an inch of iron. Ring of Many Uses 4d.*

Thirdly, there are rarer, more complex, and typically one-off items that, like characters, have Attributes, Traits, and potentially even their own equipment. For example:

> **Clockwork Knight:** *The self-declared new 'Defence Contractor' workshop of Mechanici Generali is pitching this as the future of war – an automaton powered by the springs coiled at Le Gigli, able to march for three hours or fight for one, triggered by simple binary commands played on a bugle. They may parade well, but will they be of any real value on the battlefield?*
>
> *Body 8, Mind 1, Soul 1. Mechanical Warrior 6d, Obeys Orders 5d. Metal Body (+4d), Sword (+2d).*

Finally, the Gran Meccanismo might even be considered a full NPC, if it is true that it has acquired self-awareness. Has it? Only the Guide knows for sure.

Using Constructs in Challenges

Constructs are usually used to provide bonuses in Challenges, not least because it is generally best to keep the spotlight focused on the characters. However, in some Challenges it will make more sense for a construct's Trait to be used as the base for a pool of dice. Whichever is used, the rules are unchanged. Treat the construct's Trait as the base Attribute and choose one Trait to support it, from either the construct or the player character using it, with the other effects of Goals, Flaws, and the like coming from the character. Damage in a Challenge can be applied to either the character or the construct, largely depending on what makes sense in the shared narrative.

> **Example:** *Paolo the condottiere is commanding a turtle-tank as it lumbers towards some opposing more-brave-than-smart mercenaries. It makes sense to use the tank's Lumbering Bulk 7d, especially as the Guide will also give it four automatic successes for Scale. Paolo could assist this with the turtle-tank's Revolving Cannon 7d, but he doesn't want to give the Guide a chance to say that they have run out of gunpowder, plus he wants to feel closer to the action, so instead he'll use his Cunning Tactics 5d as a supporting Trait. The tank also has Iron Armour +3d. This is not a pivotal battle, so the Guide has decided to treat the mercenaries as a single combined foe, with each one being a Thuggish Mercenary 5d and using the Outnumbered 1–4d Scene Trait, in a One-roll Challenge. The mercenaries make use of the open field to scatter and attempt to overwhelm Paolo's turtle-tank; there are ten of them, so they get +4d as a result (that being the maximum Outnumbered bonus) and a Scene Trait of Open Plain 1d. Even so, they only have 10 dice whilst Paolo has 15 dice plus 4 automatic successes, so their chances aren't looking good.*

CLOCKING

The use of clocking is largely confined to Florence and its territories. Quite how it can be used will often depend on the player's imagination and the Guide's concept of their game. Of course, the lack of a Renaissance internet – so far – will be a limiting factor. Clocking could be used to counterfeit a Catalogo identity card, to change the records in a Repeater, to access data from inside the Gran Meccanismo – although this is likely to require access to one of the workstations in the Palazzo Altoviti – or to hack into one of the dedicated cogent engines running automatic looms, metal presses, and other industrial processes. Clockers may also be able to make their own cogent engines or program or reprogram automata to which they have access. It is also worth noting that clocking entails an understanding of formal logic, mathematics, and even basic clockwork and hydraulics, so the Guide may allow it to be used in relevant Challenges, with or without a penalty.

FAITH

There is no question that religious faith can make people accomplish the extraordinary. Faith in its various guises can – like relationships, passions, and other intangible enthusiasms – be used in Challenges. It may allow a character to shrug off doubts, resist pain, inspire an army, or shame a mob. However, a Guide may also decide – not least to provide some balance against the New Science – to allow faith also to achieve effects that may seem beyond the limits of the normal. The world of *Gran Meccanismo* is not one in which priests can raise the dead or angels manifest in battle, but perhaps faith – Christian and otherwise – may be able to inspire great art, push someone on despite their wounds, and otherwise motivate people to accomplish what they, and others, thought impossible.

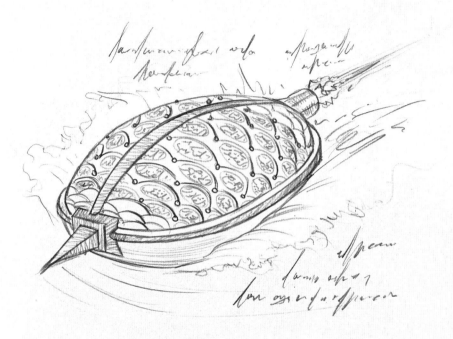

Not all New Science is Florentine. Hasan al-Rammah was a thirteenth-century Syrian chemist and engineer whose inventions, such as this sea-skimming rocket-propelled torpedo, were ignored at the time, but are now being revived by the Ottoman Empire's secretive Green Chamber.

ADVANCEMENT

People grow, people get hurt, people get old, and people learn new things, all of which is covered by Advancement. However, it is worth remembering that the purpose of play is to tell a story and have fun; *Gran Meccanismo* is not a game in which characters can quickly achieve superhuman levels of ability or where every session should lead to substantive change.

MINOR ADVANCEMENT

At the end of each game session, each player character gains a Minor Advancement. They may also gain further Minor Advancements from Flaws and completing Mid-term Goals. Each Minor Advancement lets them do *one* of the following:

- Replace a Trait with a new Trait at the same level, in keeping with the story (for example, a player may decide that, as their character has now joined the Order of St John, the Order would train them up a little, and they swap their *I Can Be Whatever You Want Me to Be* 2d for *Warrior Knight* 2d).
- Replace an existing Goal with a new Goal, even if it is not fulfilled.
- Remove a Doubt Trait from a Goal.
- Delete a Trait with a value of 1d and raise another from 1d to 2d.
- Add an extra Nudge for the next session (after the Guide has refreshed them).

For two Minor Advancements, the player can do one of the following:

- Take a new Trait with a value of 1d.
- Increase a Trait from 1d to 2d.

Minor Advancements cannot be 'banked' – if they are not used, they are lost. Yes, that does mean that if, for example, you want to take a new Trait at 1d, you'll need to use your Goals or Flaws to earn an extra Minor Advancement during the session, engaging yourself more directly and taking more risks.

OPTIONAL RULE:
IMMEDIATE ADVANCEMENT

The Guide can choose to give Minor Advancements for Flaws and Goals immediately in the course of play rather than waiting until the end of the session. This is particularly suited to a convention or other one-shot games, under which Advancement, and the rewards for goals and flaws, would not otherwise come up in play.

SIGNIFICANT ADVANCEMENT

At the end of an individual scenario, often lasting several sessions, each character gains a Significant Advancement, with another for the completion of a Long-term Goal. Receiving one of these lets them do *one* of the following:

- Take a new Trait with a value of 1d.
- Increase a Trait from 1d to 2d, from 2d to 3d, or from 3d to 4d.
- Increase Wealth by 1 (to up to 5d), assuming the Guide rules that in-game circumstances allow.

Significant Advancements can be 'banked' for the future, as they can also be used in the following ways:

- To refresh that character's pool of Nudges during play.
- Once you have banked three, to use them together as one Major Advancement.

MAJOR ADVANCEMENT

At the end of an arc consisting of several scenarios, or with the accomplishment of a World Tilt (p. 163), each character gains a Major Advancement. A Major Advancement lets them do *two* of the following:

- Increase a Trait from 4d to 5d, 5d to 6d, or 6d to 7d.
- Increase an Attribute (Body, Mind, or Soul) by 1. Each attribute may only ever be increased by a total of 3 from its starting level.
- Increase Wealth from 5d to 6d or from 6d to 7d, assuming the Guide rules that in-game circumstances allow.

Major Advancements can also be 'banked' for the future, whether to be applied during play (with the Guide's approval) or to raise a Trait beyond 7d in accordance with the Legendary Traits rule below.

LEGENDARY TRAITS

Legendary Traits are any that have a value greater than 7d. Once a Trait has been unlocked as a Legendary Trait, it can be further increased by the Guide at significant moments, in discussion with the player. These increases fall outside the Advancements covered above, but will probably require a Significant Advancement or a Major Advancement, as well as some unique story opportunity. It is suggested that only a single Legendary Trait is allowed for each character, and that it only comes in circumstances which merit, well, legend. (Yes, some of the NPCs in the book may have more than one, but they are truly extraordinary figures, such as Leonardo da Vinci.) This will then be a signature Trait for the character. Legendary Traits can be increased to a maximum of 12d.

Taodra Śä'ala claims simply to be an Ethiopian trader, selling gold, carved ivory, and civet musk from her distant land. Might she also be an emissary from Emperor Dawid II, assessing whether any of the Italian states might be a potential ally?

TURNING THE WORLD

Gran Meccanismo is set in a time of ferment and revolution. There is the clockpunk revolution of the New Science, which may liberate humanity from drudgery and superstition or usher in a new age of hydronetic tyranny and conformity. There is also a religious revolution, as the Papacy begins to face its critics and a certain Martin Luther works on his doctorate of theology. There is *also* an artistic revolution, as a generation of artists, writers, sculptors, and thinkers redefine how people think of and represent the world. There is *also* a social revolution, as old distinctions and hierarchies are brought into question. There is *also* an economic revolution, as the new power of the bankers and mercantile classes begins to challenge the old elites of the landed aristocracy. There is *also* a military revolution, driven by the New Science and the emergence of gunpowder as the defining technology of the battlefield. There is *also* a political revolution, as urban councils and feudal princes compete and coexist. And behind all these, there are the constantly changing wars and alliances between the city states and principalities of the Italian peninsula – and the looming threats of France to the north-west, Spain to the west, the Holy Roman Empire to the north, and the Ottomans to the east.

This smorgasbord of revolutions should always inform games of *Gran Meccanismo* – that sense of a world in crisis, yet also up for grabs. However, quite how much of a role it plays is up to the Guide and the players. It can simply be a dynamic backdrop, there to add colour, justify the missions the players are sent on (in games that follow that kind of structure), and add complications whenever the Guide sees fit. Sieges and wars may break supply lines, so those goods you wanted to buy might be more expensive or simply unavailable. That quick escape with the duchess's stolen necklace might become more difficult because of the riot that has broken out between the Guelfs and the Ghibellines. Having a French accent might have been an engaging aspect of your character yesterday, but now that the news of Louis XII's invasion has broken, it means those officials who need to give you your trade licence aren't looking quite so friendly.

However, it may well be that players want not just to witness these changes, but to help shape them, and here are some suggestions as to how to handle that.

NARRATED

This can be handled on an entirely informal basis. The characters may set out to bring about changes to the wider world, and the Guide can narrate the process: 'By sinking the Spanish warship, you manage to ensure that the supplies of gunpowder make it to the rebels in Sicily, so there is still a chance they will succeed.'

PLAYING AN EPISODIC ARC

The world rarely changes overnight. If the Guide and players want to make this a more central element of play then perhaps each session, or series of sessions, takes place during a different season, or even subsequent years, with the rest of the time assumed to be spent making money, training, politicking, or whatever else the player characters do. That way, there is time in between for history to unfold. Each series of sessions could be built around a different historically impactful event, such as a war, a succession crisis, or a dynastic marriage, with the consequences of the players' actions shaping the outcome, as well as playing a part in determining the nature of the next major historical event to hit Italy. This way, a game could start in 1510 and, over the course of weeks or months of play, find itself in 1520!

Of course, in this case, the Guide may want to ensure that the characters age and change over time, gaining new Flaws but also perhaps becoming richer, more experienced – and even, dare I say it, wiser.

LEONARDO DA VINCI

Da Vinci was always different, his attention flitting from art to anatomy, engineering to invention. Did Machiavelli do him a favour when he recruited him as First Technologist of the Republic? He now seems obsessed with the capabilities of the New Science, heedless of the potential human costs of his savage weapons, or of the potential for tyranny in hydronetics. He now neglects his artistic past and scarcely leaves his workshop, located in a heavily guarded and murderously trap-laden basement of the Bargello, except to consult the Gran Meccanismo or to field-test some new creation. Sporting an unusual and mysterious ocular to replace the eye he lost in a laboratory explosion, he is a disconcerting sight, his remaining organic eye seemingly always fixed on a future that only he can see.

Body 1, Mind 6, Soul 4. Artist of Every Kind 9d, Inventor Extraordinaire 12d, Obsessions Beyond Mortal Ken 7d, Disconcerting 6d, All-seeing Ocular +4d

TILTING THE WORLD

The core game mechanic can also be pressed into service to provide a kind of 'meta-game' underpinning regular play. Allow the players to set a major objective they would like to see accomplished, such as *Unite Northern Italy under Florence* or *Bring Down Pope Julius,* and then discuss a series of five to ten developments that may advance that cause, each of which is itself likely to be a major event. Then put them in a tentative order, even if real life is rarely so neatly linear.

Example:
Unite Northern Italy under Florence

1. Support for the New Science spreads in northern Italy.
2. Successful uprising in Milan brings to power a ruler friendly towards Florence.
3. France is persuaded to stay out of Italy.
4. Milan and Florence unite.
5. Pope Julius II is blackmailed into not intervening north of the Papal States.
6. Venice is forced to join the new union.

Obviously, each of these contributory events represents a massive change in the world, and one that could take months or years. They could also happen in a different order, and alternative developments could lead to the same outcome. It's important not to get bogged down in this kind of detail, but instead to treat this as an inspiration for play, rather than a script or flowchart to follow. The characters may themselves decide to act in ways that will push forwards this objective, such as by helping Milanese rebels or following up on the rumours about the embezzlement of Vatican funds by one of the Pope's closest allies. Alternatively, the Guide may, from time to time, introduce story elements that would further this long-term objective. (An especially wicked Guide may choose to place dilemmas in their path – what if the player characters' immediate interests actually run counter to achieving their long-term goal? For example, what if a character's attempt to set up a bank depends on the current Milanese regime remaining firmly in power?)

Whenever a story or a session concludes in a manner that would seem to advance the cause significantly, the players gain a die. Whenever doing so seems to coincide with one of the key events they've outlined, they can try to use the dice pool they have built up in a simple One-roll Challenge against a Difficulty set by the Guide, typically 6, to push events over the edge. There is no scope to use Attributes, Traits, Nudges, or other influences to affect this roll.

If the players lose, they simply lose their dice pool and have to build it up again. (They have to use all their dice every time they try, no hedging allowed!) If they succeed then either the intended event or something else that similarly advances their cause will happen, as determined by the Guide. All the players receive a Major Advancement.

Technically, gliders are not allowed in the skies directly over the city of
Florence, but the alianti are a maverick bunch and, typically, they must
make an unauthorised run over the city to get their wings.

THE ART OF THE GUIDE

"Cunning and deceit will every time serve a man better than force to rise from a base condition to great fortune."

— Niccolò Machiavelli, *Discourses on Livy*

As the Guide, you will create the world in which the player characters will exist, exploring the stories and adventures you devise for them. Here are a few notes on how to go about performing this role, playing to the strengths of the *Gran Meccanismo* setting and system.

WHAT KIND OF GAME?

Each Guide and group will have to decide what kind of game they want to play. Some may prefer a grand, long-term scenario with a clear arc, whilst others will want a 'sandbox' campaign in which the players take the initiative and drive the story. Others, perhaps because of the challenges in finding a time when everyone can get together, prefer short, one- or two-session standalone episodes. There's also a wide range of genres in which games of *Gran Meccanismo* can be played, from clockpunk-heavy intrigue to Renaissance soap opera.

MISSIONE IMPOSSIBILE

This is an era of espionage, subversion, assassination, and disinformation. The New Science in particular lends itself to drawing on the tropes of the espionage genre. Florentine agents could be equipped with all kinds of clockpunk gadgets, whilst mighty France, the zealots of Rome, and the ruthless masters of Venice all represent powerful and sophisticated potential antagonists. This can lend itself to a more light-hearted and freewheeling style of play like a James Bond film, or else a more brooding and paranoid one – your own *Tinker, Tailor, Soldier, Spy* under Italian skies.

CONDOTTA

You could focus on the frequent conflicts that raged across Italy at the time, either as some Richard Sharpe-style rise through a particular army or by having the characters set up and run their own mercenary company, making this as much about politics and economics as it is about the battlefield.

POLITICS

This is a time of complex, and sometimes quite literally cutthroat, politics. The characters could be up-and-coming priests hoping to make it into the College of Cardinals (and maybe even get a shot at the Papacy), fixers involved in Florentine bureaucratic manoeuvres, or major players in the court of some small city state trying to maintain its independence against all comers. The multiple-times televised story of the *Borgias* – which has just played itself out before 1510 – is full of such intrigues, but it could just as easily be a Renaissance *Designated Survivor* ('the prince and his family have all just been assassinated, except for his youngest brother') or *House of Cards*.

TRAVELOGUE

The world of *Gran Meccanismo* is a fascinating one, and maybe it is worth exploring. With the player characters taking on the role of merchants, sailors, diplomats, investigators, entertainers, preachers, or explorers, the story could always be on the move, travelling the length and breadth of the Italian peninsula, and perhaps venturing even further, whether to the Ottoman court or the distant and foggy lands of King Henry VIII.

STORY SEED: THE GLASSBLOWER WHO CAME IN FROM THE COLD

One of da Vinci's acolytes is working on a new kind of cogent engine able to process data far more effectively than the first-generation machines driven by water clocks. It will require glass vessels far beyond the capacities of Florence's glassblowers. The finest glass in all Europe comes from just one place – the island of Murano – where its secrets are fiercely guarded by the Venetians. Taking advantage of the masked festivities of the Carnival, a crack team of Florentine agents, armed with the latest New Science gadgetry, must infiltrate Venice, locate a glassblower who wants to defect, and spirit them away to safety.

KEEPING IT IN THE FAMILY

Family matters, and a nice, focused game concept is to have the characters all part of the same extended family, or perhaps its retainers. This could be *Downton Abbey – Gran Meccanismo*-style, as a once-mighty dynasty tries to hold on to what they have in a time of change and crisis, or even a Renaissance *Dallas*, in which the family is the emotional, or possibly literal, warzone at the story's centre. (This was an era, after all, when family members could be not just devoted allies but also murderous rivals.) Of course, if we're talking families, this could also be an organised crime family – perhaps a clockpunk *Sopranos* or *The Godfather*, set in the shadowy backstreets of Rome.

CLOCKPUNK DYSTOPIA

A classic theme of the cyberpunk genre is the dystopian struggle between humanity and technology. There is no Matrix or cyberspace in *Gran Meccanismo* but, nonetheless, a game could focus on two separate but interconnected dangers. The impact of the New Science may seem liberal and progressive, but it carries within it dark hints of 'hydronetic despotism', as a new generation of rulers more interested in efficiency than liberty is seduced by the potential of the cogent engines to control populations with identity cards and constant monitoring. Remember, Florence still has its state farms and Le Gigli. And what of the Gran Meccanismo itself? Can it be that it is achieving its own sentience, and, if so, what would it do with it? Put the two together, and Soderini may feel he is bringing a rational new order to Italy, but is actually being manipulated by the very cogent engines he feels are his greatest tools. Inspirations could range from *Person of Interest* to *Enemy of the State*, but variations might include making the nascent intelligence of the Gran Meccanismo an innocent seeking to understand and experience the new world in which hard-hearted masters want it to design weapons and suppress free-thinkers. Another possibility is for someone, possibly da Vinci himself, to experiment with adding clockpunk technology to a soldier or lawyer, ending up with *RoboCop* or *Universal Soldier*.

BUSINESS

This is a time when fortunes are being made and lost. Having the characters be involved in trading or banking can provide an excuse to get them involved in all sorts of other activities, such as political intrigue, pushing back against gangsterish rivals, or travelling to new places to scope out or clinch deals. Indeed, the characters could be cooperating, or they could be frenemies united against their company's rivals, but feuding and backbiting between themselves to get the best deal or most impress the boss. Not necessarily *The Office* or *Superstore* in doublet and hose, but that's not to say it couldn't be.

The more Gonfaloniere Soderini works the numbers, the more convinced he is that hydronetic management theory is the key to Florence's future, and that if the needs of humanity are best subordinated to hydronetic efficiency, then that is just what the data say.

GUIDE CHARACTERS

You don't need to populate your game world full of characters at the same level of detail as those belonging to your players. NPC characters can, as has been said, be described by one simple value, or they can be rounded out to include many more Traits as you see fit. This process is illustrated below.

THE EXTRA

Many of your characters will serve a very limited purpose in the story. They may be there to make the players' characters look good, provide a useful piece of information, say one line of dialogue, or provide some opposition to the characters' schemes. These extras can be described very quickly and simply; let's take a single North African pirate as an example:

Barbary Corsair 5d

That's about all you need to have in front of you. The 5d value is the equivalent of an Attribute of about 2d, some useful equipment, and a supporting Trait to make up the total. If an extra goes 'off script' into new territory and takes on a more prominent part in the story than anticipated, then just assume that everything else they need to do and can plausibly accomplish is rated at about two dice fewer. In this example, the pirate would be rated at 5d for maritime Challenges that use some equipment; however, if standard equipment is not helpful or the Challenge falls outside his core knowledge area, you can simply drop the value by two dice or more, so he might be at 3d or lower.

Extras don't last all that long when faced with Challenges. You may decide that they are knocked out of play – surrendering, fleeing, or collapsing – upon suffering any level of defeat.

PROVIDING MORE DETAIL

If we want to flesh out our pirate some more, we could treat his being a Barbary Corsair as an Attribute, to which a few interesting and appropriate Traits could be appended. This approach is especially useful if, for some reason, he is beginning to assume a more important role in the story, perhaps appearing more regularly as someone's friend, an antagonist, or a fellow prisoner. Let's take another look at that example description:

Barbary Corsair 5d, Flashing Knife 2d, Nimble in the Rigging 3d, Shrewd Observer 1d. Rusty Old Knife (+1d), Billowing Silken Pantaloons (+1d)

He becomes a more formidable opponent, as he can add one Trait to his Attribute; so in a fight he might be able to combine his *Barbary Corsair* Attribute with his *Flashing Knife* Trait, as well as the knife itself, for 8d (5+2+1). However, he is also now a more rounded figure with other capabilities.

SIGNIFICANT CHARACTERS

There will be a number of key NPCs who are pivotal to the development of the story. It may be that they can still be treated as extras if they are essentially just distant authority figures, but if they will interact with the player characters on a significant or regular basis then they may be worth developing further. Let's return one last time to our pirate friend:

Yusuf Raus, Barbary Corsair Captain

Yusuf is an ambitious pirate captain from Tripoli who dreams great dreams – of assembling a fleet and sacking Genoa, of breaking out of the Mediterranean and travelling to the New World. But, for the moment, he is still young, has a crew of eager corsairs, and treats raiding Christian merchantmen as a glorious game!

Body 3: *Enthusiastic if Unsubtle Swordplay 2d, Infectious Grin 3d, Wiry Strength 2d*

Mind 3: *Can Manage a Ship 2d, Navigate the Mediterranean 2d*

Soul 4: *Dreams Big Dreams 4d, Follow Me! 3d, Thrill of the Hunt 1d*

Equipment: *Scimitar and Light Mail Armour (+2d), Looted Finery (+3d)*

Nudges: *1*

More significant characters should be harder for the player characters to defeat, not least sometimes by having a pool of 1 or 2 Nudges (remember, the Guide also has their own pool of Nudges). You may decide on a case-by-case basis if they may handle defeat in the same way as the player characters or be knocked out of the story after suffering a particular level of defeat or a set number of accumulated Damage Traits. You can set this level flexibly, depending on the importance of the NPC. Such characters may also have Goals, which they can employ in the same way as players.

'Milanino' is something of a fixture in Milanese society, as well known for his easy charm as for his lyrical ballads. No one would suspect he is a secret informant for those who would free Milan of Trivulzio's tyranny and French domination.

ANIMALS AND MORE

The world of *Gran Meccanismo* isn't a world of dragons and goblins (unless you want it to be), but there are all kinds of natural threats that characters may face or harness. They can often be treated as an extra, with a single stat line, but an especially formidable threat or a loyal companion may be broken down into greater detail with some Traits or be made a full 'character' with Mind reflecting animal cunning and Soul bravery.

Thus, an angry wild boar could simply be:

Wild, Wild Boar 8d

Or you could consider making a Wild, Wild Boar an Attribute, and giving the boar some additional Traits to work with:

Wild, Wild Boar 7d, *Hairy Beast 2d, Unexpectedly Fast 2d, Really Damn Stupid 3d, Wild and Angry 3d*

To compensate for adding Traits, the splenetic swine's base number was dropped slightly, but it would still be more formidable in a fight now, because it can use *Wild and Angry* 3d to support its base 7d for a full attack of 10d. You could have decided to bring the base down further to account for this, but honestly, if you're bothering to give it Traits, it ought to be boarier than the average boar.

Here are some other examples, rendered in both simple and more detailed formats:

Brown Bear 10d, *Scale 2 for strength*

Brown Bear 9d, *Furry Coat 2d, Surprisingly Fast Lumber 3d, Massive Paws and Claws 2d, Must Protect Her Cubs 3d; Scale 2 for strength*

Elephant 10d, *Scale 3 for size and strength*

Elephant 9d, *Vicious Charge and Trample 2d, Thick-skinned 2d, Never Forgets 3d, Scale 3 for size and strength*

Guard Dog 4d

Guard Dog 3d, *Snarling Bite 2d, Speedy Bound 2d, Woof! 2d, Keen Senses 1d, On Guard 2d*

Hunting Dog 3d

Hunting Dog 2d, *Follows Commands 2d, Easy Lope 3d, Keen Senses 3d*

Prototype Clockwork Soldier 5d

Prototype Clockwork Soldier 4d, *Inexorable Advance 2d, Repetitive Attack 2d, Clockwork Running Down 1d. Simple Sword (+1d), Metal Skin (+2d)*

Riding Horse 6d, *Scale 2 for size and speed*

Riding Horse 5d, *Fast Gallop 2d, Trample 1d, Scale 2 for size and speed*

Trained Hawk 3d, *Scale 1*

Trained Hawk 3d, *Soaring Flight 3d, Keen Eyes 2d, Back to the Glove 1d, Scale 1 for speed*

War Horse 7d, *Scale 2 for size and speed*

War Horse 6d, *Fast Gallop 2d, Trained to Kick and Rear 2d, Fearless 2d, Well-trained 2d, Scale 2 for size and speed*

Wolf 5d

Wolf 5d, *Bite and Gnaw 2d, Speedy Bound 2d, Howl 2d, Keen Senses 1d, Can Trot for Miles 3d, The Pack 3d*

ON CHALLENGES

The Challenge mechanic is deliberately designed to be fast and simple. However, there may be some specific situations where things get a little more complex.

ENVIRONMENTAL AND CIRCUMSTANTIAL

Fording a fast-moving stream or surviving a night on the mountainside are straightforward examples of possible environmental Challenges. Sometimes specific circumstances will arise that you may want to treat as Challenges in their own right rather than just modifiers to other contests, such as a clocker coping with the Gran Meccanismo revealing its secret sentience to them. They are almost always One-roll Challenges and should be used only when they would significantly affect the story. For example:

> A heavily laden Giuliano has just come out of a tough fight and now wants to run after the other characters. Rather than arbitrarily decide if it's possible, you decide that he must win a Challenge against a Difficulty equal to the number of rounds the fight went on for (3), plus the 2d Damage Trait he took, and his 3d armour and equipment bonus, 8d (3+2+3) in total. Otherwise, he will have to rest first, and the other characters will be without their fighter when the Umbrian brigands spring their ambush.

> Bruno has tried all his life to shield his sister, Isabella, from a harsh world. The revelation that she has betrayed him and is seeking to steal his fortune comes just as he is about to defend himself to the court against Don Pasquale's accusations. You could just treat this as a penalty in the court Challenge, but you decide that it is so shocking that Bruno must pit his Soul (3) against a Difficulty of 4 plus his relationship to Isabella (2). Luckily for Bruno, his player thinks to suggest that he uses his Buried Anger 2d in support of his Soul, and you choose to allow it, so is the Challenge is Bruno's 5d (3+2) against the shock's 6d (4+2). If he loses, he'll be going into the trial with Damage reflecting the discombobulation and pain from this betrayal, but if he wins well, you could even give him a bonus for the trial, with Bruno fuelled by his righteous outrage.

DIFFERENT GOALS

Where each side has the same, or directly opposed, desired outcomes it's easy to work out what's going on. Where two or more individuals or groups want different, unrelated outcomes it is important to structure the Challenge in such a way that makes it clear who gets to decide what the Challenge is about. Often, it's possible to reconcile two different but related goals into a single Challenge: if Alberto wants to slap Davide about and Davide wants to persuade him not to, pit Alberto's Body plus *Quick with My Fists* against Davide's Mind plus *Persuasive Arguments*.

What if they're not directly related, though? For example, a spy might be trying to find out from an innkeeper where the secret plans are hidden, whilst the innkeeper in turn is trying to distract the spy for long enough for his son to return home and deal with this nuisance. In this case, simply run the encounter as two simultaneous but separate Challenges in which neither or both could succeed: the spy notes a tell-tale nervous glance at the third barrel behind the bar, but before he can act on this knowledge, the innkeeper's burly son Carlo has grabbed him from behind and is looking to throw him out.

GROUP

Generally, it is best to try to resolve group Challenges as between two sides, each represented by a 'champion' – whether this is a fight in a back alley or a dance-off at a grand ball – whom the others are supporting, with the results affecting everyone on that side. Alternatively, if a more granular approach is called for, it may be appropriate to pair off player characters and NPCs, so that everyone has their own personal slice of the contest. Where the numbers are uneven, some will get taken on by multiple enemies, as discussed in the Different Kinds of Challenges section of this book (p. 130).

WHAT YOU DON'T NEED TO WORRY ABOUT

In Challenges, the core philosophy of the game is to allow everyone the opportunity to describe their actions as colourfully as possible, placing dice into their hands as they go. When everyone is ready, the dice are cast and outcomes emerge. That's really all you need to worry about.

The Automated Arming Sword can be used as a normal, if clumsy, blade (+2d), but when its complex clockwork mechanism is triggered, it becomes a whirlwind of flickering blades, dashing aside the enemy's sword and stabbing into his vitals. Then, after one round, it returns to its quiescent state until the requisite five minutes of rewind have passed.

THRILLING COMBAT

Combat often forms the centrepiece of a roleplaying session, but always remember that *Gran Meccanismo* is not a detailed skirmish wargame system. This section provides some additional notes on how to handle combat, which can be used as a supplement to the base guidance on combat in the Challenge section. Refer to these ideas only if they make combat more exciting or compelling, and not if they risk undermining the tone of the game or slowing things down.

KEEP IT FLOWING

Keep the descriptions and your interactions with the players moving quickly. Combat is quick, brutal, and terrifying. The interchanges between the Guide and the players should provide an appropriate sense of urgency. One of the advantages of *Gran Meccanismo* is that there aren't a lot of rules to distract from the exciting narrative flow.

Keep bonuses and penalties manageable during Challenges. Less is definitely more in this circumstance. A quick flow of description and dice-rolling is always better than fumbling around with the minutiae of multiple circumstantial modifiers. Given the seriousness of these Challenges for their characters, players will often want to maximise their advantages before rolling any dice. As you get used to running the game, you will be able to quickly apply a range of bonuses and penalties without slowing down the pace of the scene.

GUTS FOR GLORY

Most people don't want to die! At any moment, a combatant can lose the stomach for a fight. NPCs will rarely fight to the death if they feel they have a choice – feel free to have them retreat in good order, run for their lives, surrender, play dead, or otherwise try and get out of it if they feel the battle has turned against them.

Generally, players ought to feel that they have sovereignty over their characters' actions, but from time to time, especially in situations that are especially terrifying or unexpected – which need not only be the case in direct, physical combat – you can choose to test to see if the characters have the will and determination to carry on. Set a Difficulty depending on how badly the character is faring in the Challenge, typically something like 4, plus the most serious Damage Trait they've suffered. The character can then opt not to contest this and seek to leave the Challenge or change it to a non-combative one, or else pit their Soul Attribute (with any appropriate positive or negative modifiers) in a One-roll Challenge against this Difficulty. If they succeed, they may continue as before. If they fail, they suffer an appropriate Damage Trait reflecting a loss of heart.

MISSILES AND THROWN WEAPONS

Usually, it is best to keep things simple with missile combat. Most combats will either be missile versus missile or missile versus evasion or protection, but in the main it's best not to get too bogged down in details of range and the like. Sometimes, though, this is inevitable and appropriate – when a player's Assassin character draws a bead from ambush with his crossbow, it's worth making a big deal of the shot; whilst conversely, when some poorly-trained militia are firing at the player characters as they flee into the mist, it's worth making their chances slight. Generally speaking, if the shot is considered at 'long range' (whatever that may be for the weapon in question – an arquebus flies true further than a thrown knife) then apply a 2d penalty, whilst an 'extreme range' shot means a 4d penalty. You may choose to apply other modifiers based on the context; for example if the target is in light cover (-1d), heavy cover or hardly visible (-3d), prone (-2d), or immobile and caught by surprise (+2d).

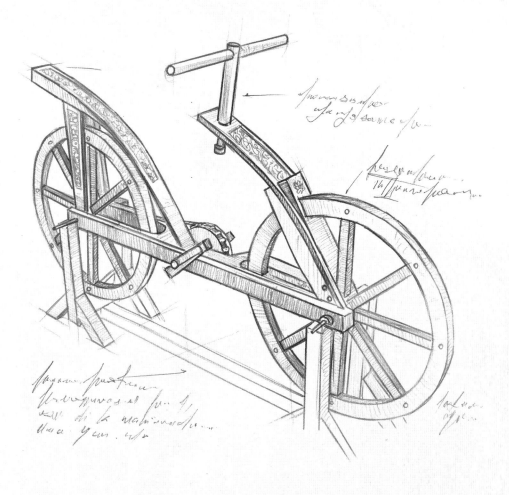

The pedal-horse has become quite fashionable in Florence, even though its cobbled streets make them a challenge for a rider's muscles and a torment for their buttocks.

THIS MEANS WAR!

This is a time of conflict, and sometimes the story your group are creating together may include big battles with hundreds, or even thousands, of combatants on each side. For example, in the real Battle of Agnadello in 1509, 30,000 French soldiers defeated 15,000 Venetian soldiers and mercenaries, killing more than 4,000 of them. There are a number of ways that you can manage this kind of event.

BATTLE AS GRIM SCENERY

If the characters are not involved in the conflict in any way, or they have no influence on its overall outcome, the battle can simply be narrated as part of the story. No dice rolls or rules are required.

ARMIES AS CHARACTERS

As discussed under Long-term Challenges (p. 132), armies can be played as rival antagonists, with ratings just like anything else. For example, at Agnadello, France's *Field Army* 8d, with the additional Traits *French Cannon* 2d and *Swiss Pikemen* 2d, was facing off against the *Venetian Army* 6d, which sadly was suffering from the Flaw *Divided Command* 1d.

If the characters are soldiers in one or both of the armies, they can offer one helping Trait to reflect their role in the battle. Perhaps they are fighting in the ranks, preparing fortifications or spying the enemy's flanks? To even things up a bit, you can add one die to the opposing army for each player character taking part.

Each opposing army may further make use of circumstantial bonuses as described by the players or Scene Traits. At Agnadello, it was *Raining Heavily* 2d.

The battle could be resolved as a One-roll or Multi-roll Challenge between the two armies, depending on how pivotal it is to the story and what the mood of the table is like. Agnadello was, in effect, a Multi-roll Challenge. In the first round, the French had a minor success, harrying the Venetian rear-guard. In the second round, as the French threw their pikemen into an attack, the Venetians were able to count on the rain to hold them off to a draw, but in the third round, numbers won out and the Venetians suffered an emphatic defeat.

Characters will share the fate of their army. If they are on the winning side, they will gain some spoils, maybe a Minor Advancement, and an opportunity to move the story along in their favour. If they are on the losing side, however, they will suffer damage. Exactly what form this takes will depend on how they participated in the battle and could be applied to Body, Mind, or Soul, be it as physical wounds, mental trauma, or becoming a wanted deserter. It's useful here to have the players describe their actions and intent during the battle before the dice are rolled – thus, when the outcome is determined, everyone can reflect on how their actions influenced the result.

CAPTAINS AND COMMANDERS

If the player characters are involved in commanding the armies, start with the opposing generals' selected battle-command Traits, with their armies providing a bonus as per the standard equipment rules (and in extreme mismatches, perhaps even adding in a Scale advantage), with the usual modifications for Scene Traits and the like.

Again, these combat rules may be used for other kinds of challenges, whether a contested election in which the characters are supporting one of the candidates (or *are* the candidates!) or a rough-and-tumble football match.

SOUND AND VISION

Your world will come to life through the words and pictures you use to describe it. The tone and mood of your game will be evoked through word choice and pacing. Make use of the plentiful source material that you have at your disposal – beyond the (admittedly significant) changes brought about by the New Science, the setting is broadly the historical Renaissance Italy of 1510. There are online resources, textbooks, novels, and more at your disposal, with rich descriptions of notable people and places, illustrations, and everything from recipes to chronicles. Sample descriptive phrases from the literature of the time to use as Traits. Play Renaissance music as a soundtrack. Show pictures from the grand masters to illustrate a scene. Props of one kind or another, from a floor plan of the church where the climactic fight is going to take place to the letter from the bishop that led them there, are always welcome but shouldn't be considered necessary, as imagination and the power of words should never be underestimated.

There are also films and TV series that can either give you plotlines and inspiration, or provide you and the players with a visual introduction. *Da Vinci's Demons* (2013–15) is especially useful, as it nods in the direction of the fantastical New Science, as do the *Assassin's Creed* short films, and, indeed the original *Assassin's Creed II* computer game. The TV series *Medici* (2016–19) and *Borgia* (2011–14) are often rather overly dramatic, but they are effective portrayals of the politics and passions of the time. *The Agony and the Ecstasy* (1965) is rather dated, but its portrayal of Pope Julius II and Michelangelo nonetheless offers a different perspective. And there is so much more on which to draw that there isn't space to get into it all here.

PROPS

Speaking of props, these can often be used to enhance even the mechanical aspects of play. For example, you could use some sort of token as the currency for your Nudges, whether it be glass beads, poker chips, coins, or even sweets. As you refresh Nudges, pass over the tokens for the player to keep. As they spend them, they give them back (or eat them). Likewise, Damage Traits that are written on sticky notes and stuck to a character sheet are not only harder to overlook, they'll niggle at the player – as they should!

OSPREY TO THE RESCUE

The highly visual Osprey military history books are also potentially useful sources. *Renaissance Armies in Italy 1450–1550* is a useful primer to all the local military powers of the time, including their weapons and tactics. *Fornovo 1495* and *Pavia 1525* focus on battles that, in a way, bookend the era of *Gran Meccanismo*, whilst *Condottiere 1300–1500* is full of information on the mercenaries of the age. If your campaign takes a more nautical turn, *Renaissance War Galley 1470–1590* is invaluable (and *Lepanto 1571* is also worth considering).

RUNNING THE GAME

You'll find your own ways of running games, with your own rhythms and tricks of the trade. These notes may help, but feel free to ignore them if they don't.

THE PLAYER CHARACTERS ARE THE CENTRE

Ultimately, this is a story about the player characters and not the setting itself. As the Guide, you will want to create situations and challenges that draw the player characters into the limelight and put them at the heart of the shared story.

Your role is not adversarial to the player characters; you're not trying to 'beat' them. Instead, your goal is to create opportunities for everyone to have fun. As the player characters' biggest fan, fill their lives with danger and opportunity and, if the group story suggests it, create endings for the characters that satisfy and resolve the shared story, set up new opportunities for the group, and make sense to the owning player. There has to be a genuine sense of jeopardy, of risks and consequences, so sometimes the best service you can give a player is a chance to allow their character to go out in a blaze of glory, saving the rest of the characters, their city, or even the world! After all, the player can always create a new character, but the stories that such an end creates will live forever in the memory.

As the player characters are at its centre, the world that you have created should respond to the consequences of their actions. The setting itself will change as the player characters influence it. This could be in small ways that ripple though confined social groupings or in major ways that topple dynasties. This will depend on the type of adventures you are having and the stakes that are set for the Challenges you will play out. A dynamic setting that changes with the player characters will feel much more real and will make sense of the action that takes place at the table.

CREATE TOGETHER

The balance of creativity can be shared around the group. As the Guide, you create the setting, scenes, antagonists, adventures, and Challenges for the players to encounter. The players will create compelling and engaging characters and describe how they act together in the setting. Everybody creates.

This sense of collaboration can extend in many directions, depending on how the group wants to play. Scene and Equipment Traits could be open for improvised creation by either you or the players. Suggested Traits can be agreed, and those you approve can be used in play straight away. You will be responsible for setting the value of Traits.

To draw out these Traits, you can ask questions. Not only 'what do you do?' but also 'what does this look like?', 'what sort of mood is there in the room?' or 'how heavily protected is the duke?' Of course, you can veto the players' suggestions, especially if they are self-interested. (If the duke they plan to kidnap seems unprotected, maybe that means the players simply didn't spot the guards, or perhaps he has some other defences, or maybe the 'duke' they're looking at is just a decoy?)

MIX UP YOUR CHALLENGES

At the heart of a game are the Challenges the player characters face. These will take the story in new directions, and their consequences will drive the fiction that you are building together. Create situations that will draw on all three of the character attributes: Body, Mind, and Soul. A range of Challenges will provide a more rounded story and enable the spotlight to be shared between players whose characters have accentuated one or other of those Attributes with higher numbers and more developed Traits.

When pacing your session, ensure that all players have the opportunity to contribute to the level that they wish. Draw out the quieter players with Challenges that play to their character's specific strengths and ensure that they are developing along with the other characters as the adventures continue.

THE RULES ARE NOT THE BOSS OF YOU

The aim is to have fun and create great stories. The rules should always take second place to that. Use them when there is a Challenge, when the story reaches a point where a decision or test of ability is required and the outcome will have real consequences. The rules are there to arbitrate significant and uncertain situations. They provide a moment of tension as impressive heaps of dice clatter onto the table and successes are counted and compared.

How often you call on the rules during your session is entirely a matter of taste and pacing. You could run a highly enjoyable session where not a single die gets rolled, with play around the table moving along in a freeform manner, referencing the information on the character sheets with the odd No-roll Challenge when required. Or the dice may be in regular use as one tightly contested Challenge follows another. Use as many of the game rules as you need on any particular evening to make things fun.

Domenico is a simple farmer, who works hard all day long so that others can eat. He hears talk of strange happenings in Florence and the wars of kings and Popes, but he knows that none of that matters as much as the coming harvest.

ON CLIFFHANGERS AND LUCKY ESCAPES

The Guide is not an antagonist to the players, but instead, in many ways, is the director of the film of their dramatic exploits. When they come up with a wild and madcap scheme, it is generally most fun and rewarding to lean into it, responding with a 'yes, but…' rather than a flat 'no'. Of course, it depends on the tone of play, but also be willing to skip past the details of the rules when it seems appropriate.

Furthermore, excitement depends on jeopardy, on the risk of failure or even death. If a character makes really bad choices, simply doesn't make the cut, or – better yet – decides to lay down their life in some epic and dramatic way, then so be it. The player can always create a new character next session. However, a run of bad rolls halfway through a session may not truly merit the bleak outcome the rules would suggest. Again, the story and everyone's fun should always take precedence, and often this can be used to generate cliffhangers and new story opportunities. Maybe the character is not killed, but instead rendered unconscious and imprisoned in an enemy's keep, creating a new 'free our friend' storyline. Or he wakes up, weak and bleary, just as the mad scientist, who thought he was dead (or doesn't care), is about to cut open his skull to replace his brain with a clockwork slave-engine.

PLAY WITH KINDNESS AND INCLUSION

Pacing a session and drawing your players in is much easier if you know them and what they are looking to get out of the game. That isn't always possible, particularly in convention settings, where *Gran Meccanismo* will be played by people who've never met each other before sitting down to play. When creating a game, set out a concept to help prospective players get an idea of the tone and intent of the game so that they can decide whether or not it's for them. Share as much as is possible up front, without spoiling any specifics.

Some players will talk more than others, but it's better not to let them steal all the limelight. Make sure you bring in the other, quieter players, and ideally introduce situations that play to their Traits and interests. Ideally, everyone should spend some time in the spotlight every session. The game is fun when everyone is having fun. You can't predict what themes or content will emerge in play, so there are some excellent safety tools online, including the X-Card, a token that signals when a player has become uncomfortable with the content or direction of the game. If this is played, accept it without hesitation, and move on and away. Note the triggering situation and adapt the content to the needs of your players.

Be inclusive, be kind, and look out for each other. Have fun.

And shape a new world.

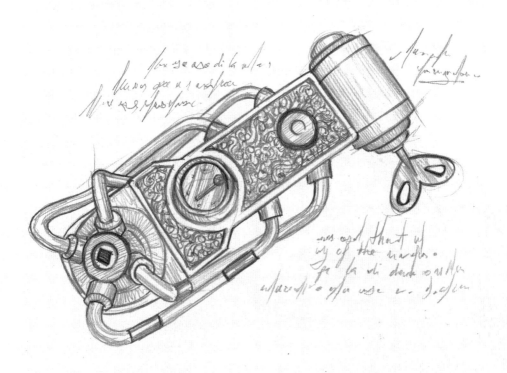

The great goal is, of course, a portable cogent engine, although such a device is presently unthinkable. The clockdrive, however, can hold data within it, to be copied from one engine to another, and this elegant one can hold twelve kilo-drips of data.

Portable Drive +3d.

APPENDIX

NO-ROLL CHALLENGES	
Number of Dice	Average Number of Successes
3	2
4	2.7
5	3.3
6	4
7	4.7
8	5.3
9	6
10	6.7
11	7.3
12	8
15	10
18	12
21	15

MARGIN OF VICTORY		
Margin	Victory Level	Damage to the Loser
0	Knife Edge	Scratch: Next roll at +1d Difficulty
1	Slight	Hurt: Damage Trait 1d
2	Solid	Wound: Damage Trait 2d
3	Major	Trauma: Damage Trait 3d
4	Emphatic	Incapacitated: Damage Trait 4d and removed from Challenge
5+	Complete	Enough to permanently remove character from play

EXAMPLE NAMES

	Female	Male	Surname
1	Adele	Alberto	Amato
2	Adriana	Alessandro	Barbieri
3	Agnese	Angelo	Bellini
4	Alessia	Antonio	Benedetti
5	Alice	Bernardo	Bernardi
6	Angela	Bruno	Bianchi
7	Anna	Carlo	Bruno
8	Arianna	Claudio	Caputo
9	Aurora	Daniele	Caruso
10	Beatrice	Dario	Castelli
11	Bettina	Davide	Cattaneo
12	Bianca	Domenico	Colombo
13	Carla	Emanuele	Coppola
14	Caterina	Enrico	Costa
15	Chiara	Enzo	D'Amico
16	Cristiana	Ercole	D'Angelo
17	Elisa	Ettore	De Luca
18	Fabrizia	Eugenio	De Rosa
19	Federica	Fabrizio	Esposito
20	Francesca	Federico	Fabbri
21	Gabriella	Filippo	Ferrara
22	Gaia	Flavio	Fontana
23	Gianna	Francesco	Franco
24	Giovanna	Franco	Galli
25	Giuliana	Gabriele	Gentile

EXAMPLE NAMES

	Female	Male	Surname
26	Giuseppina	Gennaro	Giordano
27	Ilaria	Gianni	Giuliani
28	Isabella	Giorgio	Grassi
29	Lucia	Giuliano	Leone
30	Lucrezia	Giuseppe	Lombardi
31	Luisa	Lorenzo	Longo
32	Maddalena	Luca	Mancini
33	Margerita	Luigi	Mariani
34	Maria	Marco	Marino
35	Martina	Mario	Martinelli
36	Massima	Massimo	Messina
37	Nicoletta	Matteo	Monti
38	Olivia	Maurizio	Moretti
39	Paola	Ottaviano	Neri
40	Patrizia	Paolo	Pellegrini
41	Rachele	Pietro	Ricci
42	Roberta	Riccardo	Rinaldi
43	Rosa	Roberto	Rizzo
44	Silvia	Salvatore	Romano
45	Simona	Silvio	Rossi
46	Sofia	Stefano	Russo
47	Stella	Tommaso	Serra
48	Teresa	Ulisse	Silvestri
49	Vittoria	Valentino	Valente
50	Viviana	Vittorio	Vitale

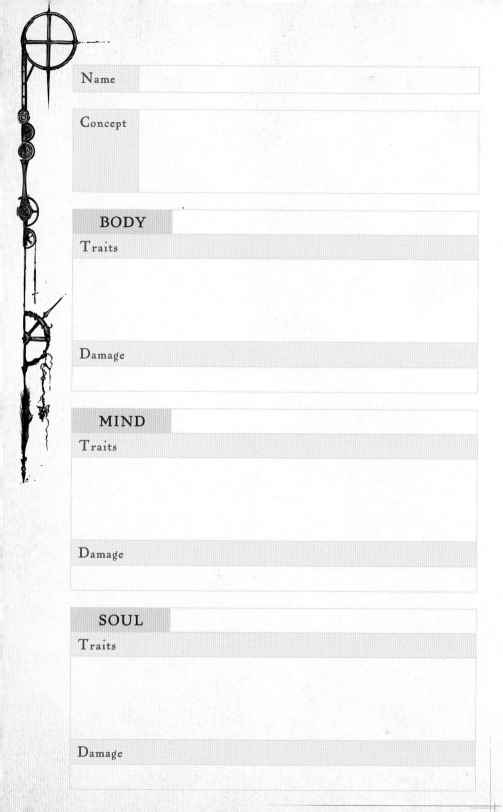

Name

Concept

BODY

Traits

Damage

MIND

Traits

Damage

SOUL

Traits

Damage

Gran Meccanismo

Age	Profession	Origin

SHORT-TERM GOALS (1D) ○ ○ ○

Doubts

MID-TERM GOALS (3D) ○ ○ ○

Doubts

LONG-TERM GOALS (5D) ○

Doubts

Completed Goals	

ADVANCEMENTS

Minor	Significant	Major

Wealth	Property
Nudges